NO

MOE SAVAGE

Order this book online at www.trafford.com
or email orders@trafford.com

Most Trafford titles are also available at major online book retailers.

Printed in the United States of America.

ISBN: 978-1-4669-7252-0 (sc)
ISBN: 978-1-4669-7251-3 (e)

Trafford rev. 02/06/2013

www.trafford.com

North America & international
toll-free: 1 888 232 4444 (USA & Canada)
phone: 250 383 6864 ♦ fax: 812 355 4082

Preface

BAD THINGS HAPPEN. WE do not live in a perfect world. It is a part of life. There is good and evil in all of us. It is up to each individual to determine how much good or evil they want to harness or keep dormant. Of course there are exceptions to the rule. Here in this we meet that exception. There are people in this world that believe someone is always out to get them. They are never able to find anything to be positive about. These type of people believe that "Payback is Hell" and are always trying to find ways to pay back the people that they believe have wronged them. I myself believe, that "What goes around comes around".

We've all heard the term "It's a small, small, world". The term simply means that one person throughout their lives will encounter the same people, events or situations in unexpected places. As you read this book, I ask that you keep this in mind.

My paramedic and police officer career spanned 25 years. Some of the experiences I had during those years were bizarre, some comical and some very disturbing. The first bad accident that I was called out to actually left me sick for 2 weeks. I have shared these experiences with friends and family and was told on many occasions that I should turn them into something to mess with other peoples' minds like I did with theirs.

What you are about to read is exactly that. I have taken those, bizarre, comical and very disturbing experiences and woven them in with a little story to take you to my own "Twilight Zone".

Just remember while you are reading this, some of the events did in fact happen. I will let you decide which ones you want to believe are real and which ones are not. Remember the famous quote from "Dragnet", "The names have been changed to protect the innocent". Maybe they have and then again.

No matter how bad your life may seem, you can always pick up a newspaper or turn on the TV and read or hear about someone that has it worse than you do. The thing I would like for you to think about as you read this book is all the turmoil, ups, and downs that this family went through. Everyone handles tragic and bad experiences in a different manner. When you finish I want you to ask yourself a question. Exactly how much could you and your family endure, and what would be your breaking point.

Chapter one

It SEEMS TO BE part of the American dream or at least in most cases where we're taught about family values, respect, and honor. Then we are taught that we have a goal in life. This goal is to go to school, graduate, maybe go to college, get a job, find that special someone, date, get engaged, get married. After your career takes off and when the time is right, you have two children. Sometimes it actually happens, at least for the most part it does. In this case two children met at a very early age, in junior high school. Their names were Jeff and Ruth. They became friends. Time progressed. In high school they were the perfect match. Everyone thought that they were meant to be together. No one else even considered asking one of them out on a date. Even their parents were sure. This would be the love of all ages.

Now we could have made another 300 pages about their lives in school. But, again in school there was nothing really exciting enough for me to write down. They had a normal life in school. Simple things like dances, ball games, homework, and your average weekend events.

They both finished high school, earning academic scholarships to the same college. Both of their IQ's were in the range of 185 which was unbelievable. They were destined to be together. Jeff went into engineering, and Ruth decided on two careers, photography and gourmet cooking. Her intelligence was off the charts. It seemed she never had to study. Jeff was exceptionally smart. Even in high school, the teachers said, if they ever had children together, the combination and genetics would be shocking. They had no idea how right they were. Again, in college it was obvious to the other classmates that they were an item. Some of the girls would even ask Ruth if Jeff had a brother. No such luck. When it came to Ruth's and Jeff's intelligence theirs was off the chart. Just to give you an idea, one question that was on the final exam, **no calculators allowed.** What is the positive solution for the following?

$2 (x - 4 - 3 \{2x - 1\} = 3 (4 - 3x) + 2 - 2x (x = 4 - 6x + 3) = 12 - 9x + 2 - x2 (7 - 5x) = 14 - 10x \ 14 - 10x = 14 - 10 \ x \ 0 = 7 = 6x - 5 - 3x$ === your answer positive solution_____

Jeff and Ruth answered the aforementioned question in less than 25 seconds correctly, using no calculator. Not one person had ever come close to this task. I'm a math freak, and my outcome was a lot longer than 25 seconds. Once again, people were sure that these two were meant to be together and with their genetics, their children would be a scary reality. Once again, people had no idea how right their prediction would be. Now for the math geeks like me, to ease your mathematical minds the answer to the aforementioned question is neither a positive or negative solution but simply -0-. Now just out of curiosity. How long did it take you to come up with the right answer? I could sit here and bore you with the activities that Jeff and Ruth had and make another one hundred pages. That would lead you right into getting lost on the essence of their story. Their lives would be changed due to life altering events that were beyond their control.

Both finished college with a 4.0 grade average. One summer afternoon they were at a very up-scale restaurant eating. Jeff looked over at Ruth. The look in his eyes pretty much said everything. Without his saying a word she said, "YES". So they were married. Jeff opened a construction company. Ruth had a photo studio and a gourmet restaurant. Life was perfect, and both were fully in love with each other. Both were very successful in their careers. The sun and the stars were definitely shining on these two. They had been married for six years. One morning Jeff left for work early. About two hours into the day, he received a phone call. Ruth was sick. Needles to say he was gone. It took him a lot longer to get home than expected. He had been stopped four times and was given four speeding tickets within just a few minutes. When he finally got home, he ran in to find Ruth at the kitchen table. She was drinking coffee. Bless his heart sometimes Jeff couldn't pick up on anything. He ran over to Ruth asking what was wrong. He never noticed the pink teddy bear or sonogram sitting on the table. When she showed him the items, he still did not understand. She told him she was pregnant with a little girl. Jeff took the rest of the day off to celebrate with his wife. Early the next morning Ruth heard a strange noise coming from the end of the hall. When she went to see what it was, there was Jeff, already working on a nursery for the little girl. He told her not to peek, it would be a surprise.

Five days later, Ruth woke up to find Jeff standing over her with a tray. Breakfast in bed," What's the occasion?" she asked.

Jeff replied, "I'm finished with the nursery". Ruth finished eating. She went to see the nursery. When Ruth opened the door, she was in major shock. Color coordinated Jeff wasn't. Everything in the room was a bright pink, really bright pink. The walls, the floor, ceiling, furniture, ceiling fan, even the door knob and light bulb were bright pink.

Ruth looked at him with a strange look, Jeff said "What?"

She just smiled and said, "Honey we need to talk. "OVERKILL". The room was changed to her specifications. Once again, life was perfect. It was as if God himself, had placed his hands on them and said, "You belong together and a good life you shall have".

Some people believe that given certain facts they can prove that family events or situations can be hereditary. Some events will reflect back on previous events. This is a small example of one such event that happened to a family member of Jeff's when he was very young. Jeff had an older brother named

Dave. One night at a party, someone slipped Dave an unknown drug in his drink. A short time later, police were called to the scene for a possible overdose. Upon arriving at the scene, they noticed six people on the front porch laughing and pointing at another man in the yard. It was Dave crawling around on his hands and knees, crying like a cat. Dave thought he was really a cat.

When the officers got out of their car, one replied, "Well I wonder which one it is".

The other officer replied back, "Do you think it might be the one out in the yard". As they approached Dave, he rose up and looked at the two officers. The officers noticed a yellow substance covering the front of his face.

He raised one hand towards the officers, folded his hand like a claw and cried "meow, meow, meow, meow, and hissed at them like a cat. According to the people on the front porch, Dave had eaten at least twelve of the little "yellow butterflies" that fly around in the yard. Dave actually thought he was a cat. They tackled Dave, handcuffed him and took him to the hospital.

On the way one officer replied "Wouldn't it have been funny to see a big dog walk in the yard and watch Dave try to climb a tree". After everything was said and done Dave was taken to Birmingham Alabama and put in the basement in a rubber room. Now, whether or not this is one of those hereditary moments or that will reflect upon the situations later mentioned in this book. Well, you will have to decide for yourself. Dave's mind was fried. He would never leave the facility alive. Thirteen months later Dave expired. A nurse found Dave lying dead on the floor.

Dave still believed he was a cat, as bad as it sounds, Dave had choked while trying to eat a live rat that he had cornered in his room. The rats bone had lodged in his throat. Part of the rat was still visible hanging from his mouth. Due to the horrific scene, no pictures were ever taken. This was a good thing.

Jeff's company was doing really well. Jeff had a couple of workers named Ralph and Shane. They were always fussing with each other. Jeff's company had another opening to fill. Craig, one of the full time employees, recommended one of his friends, a man named Ray C. On that recommendation Ray C was hired. During the first day of work the boss told Craig to get Ray C to help on a special project.

Craig shouted at Ray C and said, "Hey skillet head, I need you to come and help me".

After finishing the detail Ray C went back to his detail. Bill walked up and asked Craig, "Why did you call Ray C skillet head"?

Craig replied, "Years ago Ray C Used to have a bad habit of coming home every Friday night very drunk". Ray C's wife repeatedly asked Ray not to come home drunk. But, to no avail. Early one Saturday morning the police responded to a 911 call about a body lying on the front porch. Upon arriving at the scene, they noticed a body lying on the front porch face down. After rolling the body over, they noticed two things. One, the body was Ray C. They had recognized Ray immediately because they had arrested him on numerous occasions for driving under the influence or DUI. The other thing was that there were two teeth lying on the porch next to Ray C. They were his. His face was badly swollen. It was obvious his nose was broken and he had two very black eyes. They called the ambulance. Ray C was admitted to the hospital for a slight case of pneumonia and a concussion. The officers noticed a strange mark on his forehead. They finally got Mrs. Ray C to come to the front door. They asked her what happened.

She said, "I've asked him not to come home drunk. So I wanted to get his attention and get my point across".

One Officer asked," Did you hit him?"

She replied, "Yes, and with both hands just as hard as I could".

One officer asked, "What did you hit him with". She reached over on the coffee table and showed them. You could see the indention of Ray C's face on the back of this very large iron skillet. The funny part was the markings on the back of the skillet were the same marking on Ray C's forehead. The marking read **"Corning"** in plain letters. Corning is the maker of the skillet. After Ray C came home and until this day he never drank again. I guess he got the message. That's how he got his name "skillet head". If you look real close, you can still see the scar on his forehead that still reads Corning. Someone made the statement, so I guess he got the message. The officer said you better believe he did. It was stamped on his forehead.

On the third day of his work, Ray C's wife showed up to bring him lunch. When she got out of the car, three of the men sitting on the stairs were astonished at her size. She was what might be considered extra, extra healthy. One of the three men made a remark about her size in a real low voice to the other two. He remarked, "Man as big as she is, it would not surprise me that when she goes to the bathroom she has a good chance of getting "**Vapor locked**" when she sits on the toilet". They did not know Ray C was standing just inside the building with the door open. He heard every word. Their comment made Ray C angry and embarrassed. He confronted Craig about having a big mouth. You see, no one knew that three days prior to this Craig was over at Ray's for dinner and to watch a ball game. Little did they know that when Ray C's wife went to the bathroom, she did in fact, get "**vapor locked**". Rescue was actually called to the scene to assess the situation and finally release her from the toilet. Craig tried to explain that he had not said anything about the incident, but Ray C would not hear of it. Ray went upstairs and told on the three men. They were called to the carpet, and behind closed doors if any action was ever taken, then no one knew what it was.

Ray C had been working for the company for only two weeks. From the start he gave some of the other employees the impression that he was going to be a brown noser and a tattle tail. In the short time he had been there, he had already cried wolf on at least four other people. Several people were talking in the break room about this new employee. Someone brought up the idea it was time for Ray C, tattle tail, to get it out of his system.

Later that day, about two hours after lunch, Ray C began making very frequent trips to the bath room. On his last trip he did not make it. He had messed all over himself. Crap was actually running down in his shoes and on the floor. Needless to say Ray C took off the rest of the day.

At some point during the first break the next morning, Bill walked in the break room and wanted to know who had been using his Visine eye drops. At that moment, one of the employees pointed to Bill with one hand and with the other finger pressed against his mouth. Bill said, "What".

The employee said, "Someone had squirted the Visine eye drops in Ray's drink yesterday during lunch to get back at him for his big mouth".

Bill replied "So what".

The employee told Bill that there are certain ingredients in Visine eye drops that when ingested by mouth it would give that person a severe case of diarrhea. That's why Ray C had a bad case of "bathroom blues" yesterday. A couple of employees started laughing. No one knew that Ray C was standing behind the cubicle just a few feet away. Ray C went running to tell the owner Jeff. Jeff said he would look into it. Nothing was ever done about the incident. This made Ray C very mad.

At that point Ray C became hateful and rude to everyone until he heard Ralph and Shane arguing with each other. This continued the whole day with increasing animosity. Ray C was expecting them to cut loose on each other at any moment. It wasn't long before lunch time. In the break room all the chairs were full, except for one chair that just so happened to be the one empty between Ralph and Shane. So Ray had to squeeze in. There was just enough room to sit down. You had to go in and out single file.

Well, Ralph and Shane started at it again. Ralph was peeling an apple with his knife. Shane looked over at him and said, "Hey Ralph, what time are you going fishing this afternoon"?

Ralph replied. "Why, and why is it any of your business"? You could tell Ray C did not like his seat.

Shane shouted. "So I can come over and play with your wife".

Ralph replied, "You dirty SOB". With one quick motion Ralph took his knife, reached over Ray C, and stuck the knife in Shane's leg and left it there. Shane screamed. Due to the tight squeeze between the table and the wall, Ray C had no room to get up. So he just sat there screaming with his arms waving back and forth like he was doing the back stroke in the pool. He screamed, "hu hu hu hu". Well somewhere between the fifth and sixth "hu", Ray peed on himself. He finally cleared the table, freaking out, and ran to the bathroom. When he came back, everyone in the break room was laughing, including Jeff the owner.

See no one told Ray C that Shane had a prosthetic leg, and that Ralph and Shane were very good friends. This made Ray C very embarrassed and very angry. He left work and never came back. As he was leaving, he cried, "I won't forget this. Remember, Pay back is hell. You haven't seen the last of me". After a few weeks, all was forgotten. It was all forgotten as far as the people in the break room were concerned. Life went back to normal.

A short time, later Jeff's company acquired the contract to clear and build a gasification plant in a nearby area. One of the things that had to be removed was an old cemetery. A gentleman, dressed in a suit, was writing the names on the graves the dates and other needed information for the relocation process.

Back years ago it was nothing for wealthy to bury valuable jewelry along with their family. They had been admiring the variety of gold and other gems as they were digging up the remains of those deceased. Jeff's company had hired four black gentlemen for the grave digging. Heavy equipment was not allowed, in order to preserve the remains of those buried. They cleared the graves one by one. They reached one grave that stood out from the others. On the front of the tomb was the picture of a really beautiful young lady. By the dates of birth and departure she appeared to be in her early twenty's. They finally reached her remains. As they were admiring the beautiful gold rope with a diamond locket that had been placed around her neck at the time of her burial, they noticed a blank white piece of paper with no picture enclosed inside the locket.

At that moment one of the black gentlemen made a not so respectful comment, which we won't repeat, about the young lady in. At that instance, an image of a beautiful young lady started forming on the blank piece of paper inside the locket.

One gentleman shouted. "Oh lord, you have done made her mad and she's coming back". All four gentlemen with one motion cleared the grave. Three of the gentlemen headed toward the car. The gentleman who had made the remark was headed across the field.

They shouted, "Where are you going?"

While in a full stride he shouted back to his three friends, "The car can't move fast enough for my black butt. The three gentlemen were able to catch up with their friend as he was making the turn on the main highway some three hundred yards down the road.

As for the other people at the grave site, they were backing up due to the situation at hand. They stopped what they were doing. This freaked them out as well, making them extremely uneasy.

Jeff decided to call a film company to see if he could get an explanation for the surprising event. According to the film company, back in earlier days, referring to the date on the grave, the paper and material used was not the best quality as what is being used now. The picture had been in the dark so long that it had lost it's exposure. So, when the sunlight hit the paper, it was a crude way of redeveloping the photograph. Even with that being said, it took some serious persuasion for anyone to return to the cemetery. With the exception of the four black gentlemen who never returned. Just so you know the name on the tomb was Angel. She had died giving birth to a little girl. The reason for her death was while in her eight month of pregnancy, she had been savagely beaten and raped. From the injuries sustained during the attack, she developed complications, which were the reason for her death. Now, for the "Small world effect". It was later determined that Angel was the great, great grandmother of Ray C the former employee of Jeff's construction company. This was determined through the process of trying to return the jewelry back to the families of those buried in the cemetery. Remember the small world affect. Could this be one of them?

Chapter two

THROUGHOUT HISTORY, THERE ARE written documents where people have done horrific things to other people and animals. Psychiatrist refer to these people using all kinds of names. One of these names is a psycho-path. Priest have another name for them. They are called the **Devil**, or just plan evil. I will let you draw your own conclusion.

One night Jeff came home to find Ruth had been savagely beaten by an intruder. She had sustained numerous injuries to her face and abdomen. She was nine months pregnant. During the investigation the only things found missing were her social security card and her driver's license. According to police, in some cases the perpetrator will take these items as a reminder and trophy to reflect back on the crimes they committed. The police told Jeff to rest assuredly. These items would eventually turn back up and usually involved another crime. But, if these items turned up before hand, they would let them know.

After being released from the hospital, she became weak and very ill with pain in her abdomen. She was rushed to the hospital. Upon the exam, it was decided to induce labor. The family waited outside patiently in silence. A little girl was born. She was actually crying when the doctor delivered her. She was the picture of health.

The doctor shouted, "Hold on, I believe we have an unexpected surprise". The next thing they knew he was delivering a little boy. At first, they thought the little boy was dead. There was no sound no movement. His eyes opened. Still without crying, the little boy just stared at the nurses. His eyes were pitch black. There was not even the slightest hint of an iris, just a black mass. They looked like **death**. It gave the nurses a cold chill just to look at him. His skin was solid white, without the least hint of color. The first thought the doctor had was Albino. He never voiced this out loud. If you had filled out an APGAR just on appearance alone, the little boys score would be zero. He was so small that they could not believe that he was even alive. The doctor said that he was the smallest new born that he had ever seen. His skin was cold and clammy to the touch. Nothing about the little boy was normal except that he was breathing. At no time did the little boy ever make a sound.

All of a sudden the doctor shouted, "She's crashing". She was bleeding extremely bad from the delivery. After starting two lines of lactated ringers and a high flow of O2, she became more stable but not out of the woods. She would not stop bleeding.

After they got her stabilized they were able to go inside her and see why. They were shocked. Inside her stomach she was ripped as if someone had tried to claw their way out. After emergency surgery and countless stitches they stabilized her enough to move to a private room.

During all this time the little girl appeared healthy and happy making all the noises that a normal baby should make. But, the little boy never made a sound. All he would do is stare. His eyes remained solid black with no emotion. The entire time in the hospital he never cried. When it came time for the nurses to feed the babies, the little girl was the first one they picked up. The little boy was another story. During feeding time no one wanted anything to do with the little boy. The nurses would draw straws to see who would be stuck with the little boy. Even then some of the nurses would say that they had fed the little boy when in fact they never even checked on him at all. The bottom line is the nurses and staff was terrified of the little boy. Since the little boy didn't cry no one would know.

This went on the entire time the two children were in the hospital. The nurses figured since the little boy never made a sound no one would know if he had even been fed. No one wanted to pick him up. The nurses said the mere sight of him made them sick. The word got out in the hospital about a child that was basically a freak of nature. Everyone wanted to see the baby. The first look was enough. It did not take long before the other mothers wanted their babies nowhere around this child that looked like death. The hospital received so many complaints that they had to move the little boy to an isolated room. Whenever Jeff asked about Nathan being moved to an isolated room the nurses would tell him it was a safety concern due to his unusual condition.

From the start the nurses and hospital staff made remarks and called him names like freak, dead boy, snow flake, because of the color of his skin, and his dark dead eyes. In fact they had too many names to mention. The little girl was given the name Angel. So it was written on her birth certificate. The little boy was given the name Nathan. So it was written on his birth certificate. Well almost. Whether a typo, or on purpose, or other unknown powers to be. On his Birth certificate, he was given the name **Natas.**

Only one person noticed the spelling on the certificate. But, that was not the strange part that made her feel creepy. She noticed that when holding the birth certificate up facing a mirror Nathan's name read "**Satan**", pretty freaky huh. We'll never know how this came to be. Four days later after the nurse filled out the birth certificate she was killed in a strange accident. While attempting to revive a heart patient the defibrillator shorted out and killed her instantly. No one would ever notice this misprint until years later. The birth certificate was never changed. The nurses blamed Nathan for their friend's death.

Finally the day came to take the babies home. Everyone in the hospital was glad to see this little boy go. Numerous family and friends waited at the house to welcome the two new members to the family. As the car pulled up in the driveway, everyone was excited to see and hold the two babies. When the parents walked in, the first baby seen was the little girl. Everyone wanted to hold and kiss this little Angel.

The little boy was brought in by his father. Everyone rushed to see him. When the father pulled back the blanket to show off his son, a silence hit the room. Family and friends started backing up.

One family member commented, "There is no way in **hell** I'm about to hold that thing!" Neither did anyone else. It would appear that this would be the life set forth for the parents. The little girl would be held with open arms. The little boy would be shunned from society as an outcast. During the brief visit the little girl was the center of attention. The little boy was never held, other than by his parents, the little boy was never acknowledged.

His eyes would make your skin crawl. There is really no way to describe the exact feeling, because you would have to hold this child to remotely understand. Everybody wanted to hold the little girl. She was laughing and making all kinds of cute little noises. The little boy just stared.

For the next few years, it seemed impossible at times. You see whenever Jeff and Ruth wanted to go out with other adults or by themselves, it was impossible to do. They would look for a baby sitter. When the baby sitter would come in they always noticed little Angel. But when they saw the little boy Nathan, well a lot of times, the baby sitter would just look and say, "You've got to be joking. I'm not staying here with that freak". A few times the baby sitter would look at Nathan and just turn around and leave and not say a word. Whenever Jeff or Ruth would take the children out, they did notice one thing that seemed a little strange and unusual. They noticed that whenever they would go down the street or pull up to a red light or stop sign, if another car pulled up next to them, and there were any type of animals in the car or someone walking their pet, they noticed that the pets would stop and curl up into a ball and turn their heads away from them. It was as if the animals could sense something wrong or evil was near.

As the months passed, everything was normal when it came to Angel. She learned to talk and walk on schedule, and when she went to the doctor's office to get her shots, she cried. Nathan learned to walk at the same time as Angel, but he never said a word. When he got all his shots, he never cried. No tears in his eyes no flinching, not anything. Nothing wrong could be found. It was just as if the boy refused to talk. When it came to the little boy, the neighbors did not want this freak to play with their children. They did not want him over at their house. The only contact the little boy ever had with any other child was his sister.

The neighborhood children and parents as well picked up just where the nurses and hospital staff left off with the name calling. But this time it was worse and more frequent. They, also included names like runt, pigmy, small fry, dimple weed. Basically anything that would refer to his size, or lack thereof. Even at the age of three he could wear clothes that might fit a one year old child or smaller. The family could not even take him to ball games, the park, or any out-side activity, especially during the day time. It was hard enough at night. People would stare, point, laugh, giggle, make faces, and rude comments.

As a surprise, Jeff decided one afternoon to take the children to a pet store. This would be the first time that they had taken Angel and Nathan out in several months. They had already checked out the pet store a few days before it was decided to get the children a pet. This might fill a void for the little boy since there were no other children allowed to play with him. When they arrived at the pet store, the little girl held her brothers hand when they walked in. Upon entering the store, the animals acted in a manner that no one had ever seen before. They became silent. They hunkered down in the corner of their cages, curled up in a ball and turned their heads away from the two children. Even the snakes were acting different. They were pressed up against their cages and standing straight up as if they were standing at attention. This caused the other people inside the store to vacate in a hurry. Something was not right and it only took one look at the little boy. Trying not to cause a scene, the store owner asked if they would take the little boy outside.

When the parents left the store with the little boy, they met a police officer with his K-9. The K-9 lay down on the sidewalk and begin to curl up. This was strange. The K-9 had never acted like this. Angel took her brothers hand and walked towards the dog. The dog messed all over himself and started crying, It was as if the dog thought he had been shot and died. The officer was in a state of disbelief. When the officer told the other officers about the incident they didn't believe him. It took several minutes for the pets in the store to return to normal. As far as the K-9 it was several hours. It appeared as if the K-9 had been singled out. Whether the little boy touched him or not is still just a guess. Even the neighbor's pets on each side of their house would act funny. Whenever the two children would go in the back yard and play, the dogs and especially the cats would run to the other side of the house. It didn't take long for word to get out throughout the area. They fenced in the back yard to keep the neighbors and on lookers away from their children. Jeff decided this was the best way to protect the children. So be that as it may this would appear to be their life.

Have you ever noticed it's a small world and how some occurrences and events reflect on future dates? Here again, this falls in place with events of past and present. There's an old saying, if you look hard enough, you can always find that one bad apple in the barrel. In this case, the one bad apple just so happened to be a young police officer. No one liked him. I don't think he even liked himself. He started out as part time. His name was Chadwick. A lot of people considered him to be the biggest brown nose and cry baby they had ever seen. Some say he was this way by throwing all the spot light on someone else, just to cover up his own short comings. He was always running to the chief and telling lies just to collect brownie points. He had gotten wind of a possible full time opening. He began writing excessive amounts of tickets for reasons that other officers might overlook. One example was he would give speeding tickets for going as little as three miles an hour over the speed limit. Other officers would allow fifteen miles over. When you have a job where you deal on a direct basis with the public, it's a good practice to build up and maintain a good rapport with them. For this one officer, Chadwick, his only concern was collecting brownie points. Now, that he did, he was writing ten times as many tickets as any other officer. Brownie points paid off. He was given the full time position. Now other officers wondered; how long could he keep it up. Chadwick had made so many people mad that other officers were scared to go to the local restaurant. Chadwick had written every person who worked at the local restaurant at least one ticket. Some were given numerous tickets. Even their families had been saturated with tickets. Rumors quickly spread, due to all the tickets Chadwick had written. If any officer came to eat at the restaurant, their food would have a few extra ingredients added that was not on the menu. You can only guess what those ingredients might be. Not only did certain individuals but some of the officers said if the "brown nose" Chadwick ever got in a fight or needed help, the word was the officers would not have a radio signal. Therefore, they could not respond. As far as individuals, their word was they would stop and watch. Maybe even drink a Dr. Pepper. But no way would they help for any reason under God's green earth.

Chadwick acquired a police dog. The incident at the pet store would be too much for Chadwick's ego. Three days had gone by. Chadwick was on his way to the office to pick up his pay check, just like he had done dozens of times before he was leaving his K-9 at home. He just could not take any more harassment about the way his dog had acted at the pet store. Remember, several of the other officers had no use for the brown noser. When Chadwick opened up his locker, he found a stuffed pink poodle with a note, "Here's your new partner". He went crying to the chief as usual. But no one knew about his new partner. So I guess it is a small world.

One thing that amazes me is how some lives keep interchanging with events from one moment in time to another moment in time. Three days later Chadwick and his partner get a call. The call is 2 houses down from Chadwick's house. The call is urgent. Upon arrival at the scene, Chadwick's wife emerges from the garage at the scene. His partner notices an enormous blood trail leading from the garage and continuing down the street. At that moment, Chadwick's wife approached him with tears in her eyes. When Chadwick looked down at the inside of the garage, well the expression on his face was enough said. Even through all the blood and guts, he could still recognize the collar of his K-9. It appeared someone had taken the collar and hooked it to the main vertical support beam to the garage, then took another collar or harness and hooked it to the back of the truck in the garage. The end result, well the end result was stretched from the garage to three houses down the street. The K-9 police dog was basically peeled apart like an onion, until the parts were small enough to slip through the collar. After the scene was cleaned up and investigated, neighbors came to Chadwick's house to pay their respects. No perpetrator was ever found. Sympathy cards were left by a lot of the neighbors, including one card that really stood out. The card was signed by the neighbors, five houses down the street. The card read he was a good dog, signed by Jeff, Ruth, Angel and Nathan. Another card sent by the neighbor from the street behind Chadwick. It was signed, "We'll miss him", signed by Ray C, a former employee of Jeff's construction company. So I guess it is a small world after all.

The one thing that baffled the officers was with the special training the K-9 went through. The dog would not have let another person get close enough to him and let another collar be put on him. Also, he would not have taken food from someone else. So being drugged was out of context. So the how question or why would never be answered. Rumors of course hit the neighborhood. Most of the rumors seemed to anchor towards the family down the street, Jeff, Ruth, Angel and Nathan. A funeral was held for the K-9 officer. Dozens and dozens of people showed up. Around the grave on one side stood, Chadwick, the mayor, and the chief of police, on the other side stood the rest of the officers and numerous citizens. After the funeral was over, a party was given to honor their fallen colleague. At the local restaurant, a large buffet was laid out with a picture of the k-9 over the buffet. The buffet was ready. First in line was the partner of the K-9, officer Chadwick, then the chief and the mayor. That was it. While they began to fill their plates, they wondered where everyone else was. They would have a long wait. Three miles down the road at another restaurant the parking lot was full. At the front entrance was numerous police cars and a few fire department vehicles, not counting dozens and dozens of other private owned vehicles. There at the center of the room were nine pictures of the K-9 officer. All nine pictures were from his puppy days to the last one ever taken. From this I guess you can see how well Chadwick was liked. No one ever said anything about the party being held for the K-9, nor did they invite Chadwick. Later that afternoon the chief asked the assistant chief where everyone was at. He told him the truth. No one liked the little brown noser or had any use for him. The chief never said a word. He just turned shaking his head and walked off. Chadwick was furious when the Chief told Chadwick about the other party. Well, this made Chadwick even worse when it came to brown noising or telling on other officers. He also became more ridiculous and crazy when it came to writing tickets. Needless to say, Chadwick became more hated by the other officers. He was also really despised and hated by the public. Three weeks had passed since the funeral. Chadwick was racking up more tickets than all the other officers combined.

On the Saturday morning of the fourth week, it was opening day of baseball season at the local park. Just about everyone was there, including personnel from the fire department and six police officers from the local department. The location of the park was two hundred feet from another county line. About noon a faint sound of tires screeching the pavement could be heard as a Camaro sped by the ball field with a police car hot on his tail. When a short burst of the siren echoed from the road, the Camaro stopped. The officer with his lights still flashing emerged from the car and walked up behind the Camaro. The driver got out and walked to the back of the car. As the officer pointed toward the trunk of the Camaro, it would appear the officer was instructing the driver to place his hands on the trunk; so the driver did. As the officer began his search of the driver, the officer pulled a small plastic bag from the drivers pocket.

As the officer reached for his handcuffs the two rear doors of the Camaro opened. In an instant the officer was surrounded by three men. Before he had time to react he was in a fight. As the three men began to beat the hell out of the officer people at the ball field just watched. A lady who knew the six officers at the field went and told them about another officer needing help. They took off running to assist. When they got to the back of the bleachers where they could see what was going on, they stopped. Sure enough, there was one of their officers getting the hell beat out of him. Three men were standing over him kicking various parts of his body. One of the officers said, "Hey look, it's Chadwick". They stopped, turned around, and went back to sit on the bleachers and finished their hot dogs and Dr Pepper.

When one of their wives said, "Hey, are you not going to help your friend?"

One officer replied, "It's Chadwick and we can't, he's ten foot outside our jurisdiction. We would not want him to tell on us for going out of our jurisdiction again". The three men after a couple of more kicks reached down took his badge off his shirt, his duty belt, his gun and even took his shoes from his feet. They got back in the Camaro and left. Chadwick lying on the ground bleeding and bruised from multiple areas raised his arm and with his hand motioned and waved as if to signal for help. At that point the six off duty officers stood up, raised their hands and waved back. They turned around and went back to watch the ball game. The people in the stands stood up and waved back to Chadwick then turned around, sat back down and resumed watching the ball game as well. Finally Chadwick made it back to his car. When he reached for the radio, the microphone was gone. Apparently one of the three men took it so that he couldn't call for help. Bleeding and bruised, he made his way to the hospital. It was not going to be Chadwick's Day. Upon arriving at the hospital, Chadwick hobbled in to the ER. When he walked in, the nurses turned and walked off. He approached the desk to find no one there. It was shift change. The nurses saw it was Chadwick. All of them had been given numerous tickets by Chadwick for picky things. They all pretty much agreed that the jerk could set there and bleed for all they cared. No one was willing to help. The nurses coming on duty were in no hurry either. I guess if you add it up, the short time that Chadwick had been there, his ticket frenzy had affected about 98% of the people in the city, whether it being the direct victim of a ticket or a family member or a good friend. Any way the word was out. Finally the chief got word of the incident and rushed to the hospital to check on the brown noser. When the chief looked inside the police car at the blood, he stood back and screamed like a little girl. Guess he wasn't used to the sight of blood. Rumors have it that is how the chief got his job, being a brown noser himself.

Other officers tolerated the chief, being their boss, but outside the department they had no use for him either. Chadwick finally received medical attention for his injuries. He came out ok. His injuries consisted of one broken wrist, two broken ribs, a few abrasions and bruises and one concussion. After the chief got Chadwick's statement and found out that six of his officers did not give aid to one of their own, he was not a happy camper. He went back to his office and called the six officers in. After they all arrived at the station he unloaded. After thirty minutes of screaming and shouting without taking a breath, one of the officers smiled. That did not help at all. So the butt chewing continued. The chief pulled out a piece of paper and threatened to suspend them for two weeks without pay. One officer stood up and said, "Why, you wrote us up for being just a little piece outside our jurisdiction. Now you want to do it again because we did not go outside our jurisdiction. "I don't think so".

The chief said "Hell yes".

With that one officer said, "Chief, if you do I've got one word for you, lawsuit". At that point the six officers got up and left the chief in his office with his mouth hung open. The doctor on call kept Chadwick in the hospital for two days, then he was discharged.

When Chadwick asked for pain medication and a work excuse, the doctor said, "No, you don't need it". It might be the doctor was still a little pissed for Chadwick writing his mother and Daughter a traffic ticket for parking too close to the curb. Election time was around the corner. Chadwick knew if a new mayor was elected and the chief was replaced, he would be gone. So before that happened he would resign and move to another police department. The election took place, and no changes were made, but Chadwick had already moved to another police department. The mayor and police chief retained their status and jobs.

Chapter three

Early one morning screams and cries broke the silence. The family ran outside. Nothing could prepare the family for what they saw; Angel was screaming and crying. There under the clothes line covered in blood was Nathan, just looking up. The blood and noise was from what was on the clothes line. There on the line were two of the neighbors **cats.** It appeared the little boy had tied their tails together and had thrown them over the clothes line. This was a bloody sight. The cats had clawed each other until their guts were protruding from their stomach. It was a sight that was unimaginable. When the parents shouted," Nathan what the **hell,** have you done?" Nathan just turned around with his arms stretched out and his palms facing up. Blood was dripping from his hands and fingers. Nathan just starred at his parents and never said a word or never showed any signs of emotion. The police were called to the scene. After some serious talking, the parents of the little boy paid restitution of $500.00 for the two neighbors' cats. As far as the little boy, the parents were not sure what to do. So while trying to figure out what to do. Nathan still never said a word, and, the little girl seemed to be coping with the previous event. Until, three days later, A cry came from outside the door to the house. When Jeff and Ruth ran to the front door of the house, they stopped and stood there in a state of awe and shock. It did not take long for the front yard to fill up with neighbors and on lookers. The carnage was very bad and gothic. At first everyone just stood looking. For there nailed to the door was the left over skin and complete head of another **Cat**. There stood little Nathan covered in blood, and Angel crying. The police were called. This, time the cat belonged to the neighbors on the other side of the house. The parents paid five hundred dollars to the cat owners not to press charges. This time the parents set down and decided to send the little boy to a psychiatrist.

After months of therapy the psychiatrist said that he had done everything that he could do and left it at that. The parents assumed that all was well. Early one morning Jeff and Ruth decided it would be a good idea to catch up on some much needed yard work. It would be a shame to waste such a beautiful sunshine day especially since the children Angel and Nathan were asleep. So while Ruth worked in the flower bed, Jeff worked in the yard mowing and weed-eating. They had kept both children up late the night before watching TV and eating popcorn. About twelve noon they both finished their work. They would check on the children. If all was ok, then Ruth would take a shower while Jeff picked up all the tools. When they went into Angel's room she was not there. They checked Nathan's room, he was not there. Time to get worried, they ran from room to room in the house looking for the kids to no avail. So they went out back. A sigh of relief. There was Nathan and Angel playing in the sand box. Jeff went ahead and put up all the tools. Ruth was getting ready to take a shower. Ruth closed the door and turned the shower on. When she got in the shower, she heard a strange popping sound coming from above her. So she looked up. Jeff had just walked in the house. A few seconds later, Jeff heard a loud scream and crash coming from upstairs. Jeff ran upstairs to the bathroom. Shouting, "What's wrong"?

Ruth called from the bathroom, "I'm in here, help me", Jeff burst through the door. Upon entering the bathroom, there lay Ruth on the floor crying.

With a little bit of blood on her arms and legs, he said, "What the **hell** has happened?" Still crying Ruth looked at him and pointed up at the shower.

When Jeff looked up he gasped and took three steps back in shock. After he gathered his composure, he grabbed his wife and helped her back to the bedroom. He began to check to see how bad she was hurt. By the grace of God she only had a few bruises. The blood was not hers. He looked at her and said you stay here. I'll take care of the bathroom. She did not complain. When Jeff went back into the bathroom, the popping noise was still echoing off the walls. The sound stopped when he turned off the shower. Still in shock, Jeff grabbed the shower head. A really bad chill came over him. For there mounted on the shower head, was in fact the head of a white **Cat.** When Jeff reached up and pulled the cats head from the shower, the sucking sound was bad. With one more hard pull, the cat's head came off the shower. It sounded like someone opened up a bottle of Champagne. He became really sick and started throwing up and gagging. It was not the sound that made him sick. It was the after effects of removing the cats head from the shower. When the suction gave away both eyes of the cat exploded from its head. One eye landed in his front shirt pocket. The other eye landed in Jeff's mouth which would leave him with a taste that would not soon be forgotten. After cleaning up the bathroom and still trying to cope with that awful strange taste, he went back to check on his wife. When she asked what had happened, he became sick again. Well, being nosey like most women are. She had to know what happened. So he told her. She became very sick. No kisses for Jeff. After calming down, he took the cats head and one eye. Yes, that's right one eye. He put them in a dark plastic bag and drove to a nearby creek and chunked them over the side into the water. So just in case you're wondering where the other Cats eye went. Well, good old Jeff being as slimy and slippery as the cat's eye was. **Jeff swallowed it**. After returning home, Ruth and Jeff set on the couch looking at each other and not saying a word.

Ruth asked, "Where is the rest of the cat?" They looked and searched all over the house, but to no avail. Just as soon as they sat back down on the couch, Angel and Nathan walked in.

Angel looked at Jeff and said, "What's for lunch?" For some reason Jeff got up and ran to the other bathroom. The rest of the cat was never found. Ruth and Jeff did not eat lunch, but the children did. Ruth and Jeff agreed on one thing; sometimes some things are better left unsaid. This most assuredly was one of them. It was three days before Jeff could eat again. Everything he tasted even drinking water tasted like a cat eye. Enough said. They say in time all things will heal. This isn't one of them. Well, maybe one more thing.

Jeff and Ruth were awakened early one morning to a sound that they had not heard since the birth of Nathan and Angel, the day they brought them home from the hospital. Jeff walked down the stairs to the back of the house. Once there he very slowly opened the rear door to the back yard. Yes, there it was much to his surprise. He slowly closed the door and ran back upstairs to tell Ruth what he had seen. She grabbed her gown and ran downstairs to confirm the sightings. Upon reaching the rear door with Jeff standing beside her, she very closely opened the door.

She confirmed the sighting softly whispering in Jeff's ear, "Oh my God, I can't believe it." With a gentle kiss to his cheek and a soft caress of his arm, they eased on to the back porch, closing the door behind them. Both sat on the porch swing trying not to make a sound. Both sat there in a state of awe. Not only was the sun shining, but it was the first day of spring. Now to add icing on the cake was the strange sound that had awakened them to start with. Not only did they see birds chirping, there were four squirrels playing in the sand box as well as two more squirrels playing on the children's swing set. They sat there for at least two hours enjoying the spring offerings of Mother Nature. Jeff saw a movement from the corner of his eye. He slowly turned his head to get a better look. He gently squeezed Ruth's hand and with a soft voice he told her to look to her left. For there on the porch rail sat two baby squirrels looking at Ruth. This was the best morning that they could remember having in a long time.

They say you never get a second chance to make a first impression. Within a blink of an eye, the birds and squirrels were gone. In fact the only noise you could here was the screen door closing. Angel and Nathan had walked onto the back porch. One look was all it took. Mother Nature must have sounded the alarm. Within a second the birds and squirrels were gone. One look at Nathan was all it took. Ruth and Jeff went back inside to fix breakfast while Angel and Nathan stayed in the back yard and played. After breakfast was finished, Jeff and Ruth washed dishes. Nathan and Angel were going to go back outside and play, but they turned around and came back inside to watch cartoons due to a slight rain shower. Ruth looked over at Jeff. He could still see the disappointment in her eyes. He slowly took her hand in his and escorted her outside. There she began to cry. Much to her surprise Jeff took her out into the yard and began to slow dance in the rain with her. This was a very emotional moment for Ruth. Jeff knew how much she liked dancing, but in the rain, well this was very special. Just at that moment the rain stopped. Ruth looked at Jeff and said, "Well, it was fun while it lasted."

Jeff looked at her and said, "Baby, stay right here." All of a sudden it started raining again. Jeff came back and pulled her to him and began dancing again. Jeff does have a moment every now and then. He had just compensated for the rain stopping by throwing a water hose over the top of the house. Their slow dance lasted for quite a while. Well, let's just say after the slow dance in the rain, the rest of the day and night was special as well, so special that Jeff had breakfast served to him in bed the next morning. So as I said, you never have a second chance to make a very good first impression.

That afternoon Jeff went all out. While Angel and Nathan played in the back yard and Ruth relaxed on the couch, Jeff grilled the children burgers and fixed him and Ruth the two largest Black Angus rib eyes you have ever seen. They were so huge that one cow donated her life for that meal. The burgers were so tender and juicy that Angel and Nathan had problems keeping them on the buns. The steaks were so tender you could have cut them with a rubber fork. That night while all four of them sat in the living room watching TV to and nibbling on popcorn, Jeff looked over at Ruth and said, "Honey, I just realized something."

Ruth replied, "Hush, don't say it." Both had realized that this was the first full weekend that no police, fire trucks, or neighbors had come calling or knocking on the door complaining about animal carnage or missing pets.

The first day of school was upon them. When Ruth walked in the main office of the school, there was a hush. The principal walked out, and trying not to appear shocked, welcomed Ruth and the two children into her office. After processing the two children, the principal called a teacher to her office. When the teacher walked into the office, she saw

Angel and smiled and said welcome to our school. She turned and saw Nathan. Before she had time to think, she said "What the **hell**"? The principal made her apologize for her remark. The teacher said it's time to go to the class room, and took Angel's hand and motioned for little Nathan to follow. Upon entering the class room, a silence came over the class. One child began to point and laugh. Another child and another and another until the teacher began to laugh. She instructed the two children to take a seat. When the little boy sat down, the other children in the class moved to another chair away from the little freak except for his sister.

The names started just like before such as powder puff, dark eyes, snow flake, and too many others to mention. Even the teacher got in on the act. Every time she would call little Nathan she would call him by one of the names given to him by the other children. This went on and on. It didn't take long before the whole school knew about this child. This child with dead eyes. During lunch time a special table was set up so the two children could eat by themselves. None of the other children wanted to eat with this freak. When the other children got home, they told their parents. They did not believe their children. The next morning when one of the other parents walked into the class room, that was all it took. She could not wait to call the other parents to tell them about this freak that was allowed in class with their children. To confirm this several parents visited the class room. The constant phone calls to the school office demanding that their children not be allowed anywhere near this dead eyed freak. The school assured the parents that there was nothing to worry about. Or, so they thought. The little boy would look and stare at the other children. One of the other children took goat droppings and put in the freak's chair. Everyone laughed even the teacher except for little Nathan's sister. Pranks on the little boy went on for several days. Until, the parents received a phone call from the school. Upon arrival at the school the parents noticed several police cars at the school. The principal and a police officer met them at the door and said, "We have a major problem." They walked Jeff and Ruth to the football field. On the ground at the base of the goal post, there was the school mascot, or what was left of it. There again, was little Nathan covered in blood and his sister crying.

When Nathan's parents saw what he had done, they shouted," Not again. What the **hell** have you done?" Nathan turned around with his arms extended out and his palms facing upwards. Blood was dripping from his hands and clothes.

The officer turned and said," What do you mean, not again?" It did not take long before parents and phone calls flooded the school. Words echoed from the principal's office. The word most heard was lawsuit, if something was not done immediately with that freak. The officer pulled the two police reports previously involving the little boy and showed them to the principal. It appeared that the goat had been skinned alive. How was this possible? That such a little boy could do such a horrific thing?

This time the little boy was expelled from school until another psychiatrist could re-evaluate him. For one year Nathan was kept in a mental hospital. He was allowed one weekend pass every three months. But the location was kept a secret. At home it seemed that everything was slowly getting back to normal except for the absence of the little boy. The neighbors were fine, and the school was still trying to get over the event. Angel seemed to have no emotional scars from the previous events. Two months went by and a phone call from the mental hospital where the little boy had been for almost one year. You can come see your son. Ruth and Jeff were in the process of getting ready to go get Nathan when they noticed a strange smell but could not seem to locate the source. When Ruth put her feet into one of her dress shoes, she felt something weird. When she pulled her foot out, she grabbed her mouth. A liquid was oozing from under her hand and between her fingers puke. There on her foot were some tiny little worms maggots. Stuck on her foot was the rest of the cat without its head and eyes. This again was one of these things better left unsaid. They chunked the rest of the cat.

Upon arrival at the hospital, the psychiatrist said the boy would need to be on a special medication. The medication was for psychotic disorders. This medicine would prevent such a problem from happening again. During Nathan's three month stay at the facility, the family was allowed to make periodic visits. It always seemed to help the little boy if the family visited him separately. First Jeff, then Ruth, and then Angle would visit. There were always positive signs of considerable improvement after each visit. What was really amazing was the amount of intelligence that little Nathan introduced with drawings and writings. His intelligence would appear at a twelfth grade level. His clarity of drawings were exact and precise. The parents told the doctors that his little sister had the same gift. He was given several test, and it was determined that his I-Q was in the range of 160. This was unheard of for a child at his age. After one weekend visit by the family the doctor returned and found something written on the wall. He showed the nurses which really freaked them out. This was surely not normal. Even though the majority of drawings were morbid, and some of the writings were a little odd. How could a six year old boy have thoughts and words run through his mind. The doctor thought it best that he not tell the parents or let them read these writings. He took pictures and copied them down and put them is his report. This is what the little boy wrote on the inside of the door which was written in human blood. The source of the human blood would never be found.

Behold these eyes
How lifeless how still
Destined for immortality
Destined to kill
Discerns of thoughts in life here did dwell
The final destination lustrous heaven or terrific hell.
Did startling images here find a place?
Or worship of an idol in a serpent's face
Bitterest hatred may reign supreme
But condemned soles are his eternal dream.
He spoke of silence that you would never hear
His dead black eyes would never know tears.

He was marked condemned before life ever began
For here stands before you, is Satan's kin.
He shall never feel love, hate, or pain
His sole belongs to hell, in which he will reign.
He was marked condemned before life ever begun
Welcome my friends meet Satan's son.

The doctor sealed the files in the records of lost and deceased. He wrote a notation at the bottom of his final analysis. Something will happen with this child of evil. I recommend that there is no hope. Due to his intelligence and demeanor, that in time he will most assuredly cause more pain and even probably death. He should be locked up, because I have no idea what should be done with him other than simply be destroyed. God help us **Satan** has arrived. The doctor reviewed all the paperwork on the little boy from the time of birth when something caught his eye. The one thing that no one noticed, on the birth certificate the little girl's name was Angel. The little boys certificate, whether it was done on purpose or a typo, the little boy's name was Nathan. But on the birth certificate his name was listed as **Natas.** Even the parents never noticed this when the doctor showed them a copy of the birth certificate, they were shocked. The doctor showed them something else about Nathan's birth certificate. When you hold it up to a mirror, it reads "*Satan*". Neither of them ever noticed the mistake. The doctor released the boy. The parents took little Nathan back home.

Upon arrival at their home, the neighbors kept their children clear. They didn't want their children around this little boy. By the way the name of the little girl was Angel. The name of the little boy was Nathan just in case you missed the first part. No one knew that Nathan had returned home.

It was now the eighth birthday of the two children. A big birthday party was planned for the two children. The party was to start at 3 pm. At two fifty no one was there. It seemed that no one would show. At 3:10 a couple of cars pulled in the driveway. Right behind them were two more cars a total of seven children with parents got out of the cars. Everyone came in, the party was going really well. Little Nathan walked in the room where the rest of the children were. The parents and the children stopped what they were doing. It was obvious that they were not pleased to see this freak that never should have been there. To make a fast exit, the parents said to the family. Well, it's time for gifts. Everyone dropped Angel's gifts at her feet then left. There were no gifts for little Nathan. Little Nathan just looked at the children and the parents. No sound and still not a word was ever said. You would not believe how fast the party ended. Seven children and parents were gone in a flash. They did not even say goodbye. The parents of the seven children still thought that Nathan was still in the hospital.

Jeff and Ruth did, in fact, get Nathan a brand new bright shinny new blue bicycle. The next week everything seemed ok until little Nathan's bicycle came up missing. The parents looked everywhere, but no bike was to be found. A few days later Angel told her parents she thought she had seen the bike at one of the boy's house that was at the birthday party. Indeed it was. Jeff went and retrieved the bike from the house. The owners of the property said that they had no idea how the bike wound up at their house. The boy denied taking the bike. The bike was hidden behind the bushes, not visible from the road, but it could be seen if you were walking on the sidewalk. Little Nathan was exiled from the other children in the neighborhood until time for school. For Nathan to be allowed back in school he would have to see a state appointed psychiatrist. The judge presiding over the case issued the order which was three months observation in another facility with 24 hour monitoring. There Nathan would remain incarcerated at this facility until further notice.

Chapter four

THERE IS AN OLD saying "silence is golden". Have you ever wondered what causes the silence to start with? It was early one spring morning as day broke. Grass glistened with dew from the morning sun. Birds, Squirrels, and other wild life enjoyed the offerings of Mother Nature. All at once, an ear piercing scream echoed through the court yard. The staff and visitors converged on the echoes of pain. Upon entering the courtyard, the staff and visitors stopped in disbelief. The carnage was so severe that not only the visitors but some of staff became sick and were throwing up. For there in the corner of the courtyard was Angel crying. There stood Nathan with his arms extended forward and his hands rotated with palms facing up. Blood was dripping from his blood soaked hands. The blood was not from Angel or Nathan. There above Nathan's head were two Persian cats, or what was left of them. It appeared that Nathan had taken the two cats, tied their tails together, threw them over a clothes line, and watched them claw each others guts out. Until, I guess you could say both cats used all of their nine lives in that one sitting. The live action only lasted a few minutes, but it seemed like an hour of carnage on the move. The two cats were the pride and pets of the mental facility where Nathan was incarcerated for an incident just like this. The staff was furious. They demanded immediate action. The visitors were in an up-roar. They threatened the facility with lawyers and law suits if that little freak was not immediately removed and sent to another facility. The director agreed, but it would take time.

To keep the lawyers and visitors of family currently living there satisfied, there was one place they could keep Nathan temporarily until another facility agreed to take him. This way, as far as anyone knew, little Nathan had been transferred to another facility. There was an old storm shelter stuck back on the southeast corner of the property that had pretty much been forgotten about. Maintenance put in a 30 watt light bulb and a plastic bucket for Nathan to use the bathroom in. Maintenance had taken the doors off the shelter and replaced them with iron bars two months prior to Nathan's arrival to house a couple of guard dogs. But one week before Nathan arrived they had gotten rid of the two dogs. The attendant in charge of taking care of Nathan hated going outside in the weather, so he figured if he was going to have to take care of the little creep he might as well have fun while doing so.

The attendant was a big competitor in the paint ball competitions, so he figured since no one ever went to check on Nathan he might as well use him for target practice. The attendant would go there several times a day to give Nathan his exercise. He would tell Nathan to walk back and forth from one side of the shelter to the other. While doing so he would shoot at Nathan with the paint balls. He would always shoot Nathan from the waist down. The paint balls would leave really bad bruises on Nathan's pearly white legs. Sometimes the attendant would freeze the paint balls so they would not burst. These really left bad places on Nathan's skin. To make things more interesting and to improve his skills he would take Nathan out of the storm shelter and to a group of trees farther behind the shelter where he had installed a line between the trees. Nathan would be handcuffed to the line but he would still be able to run between the trees while the attendant used the other trees as cover while shooting at him.

Considering how small Nathan was, the one thing that always amazed the attendant was no matter how many times he would shoot Nathan with the paint balls or how bad the bruises were, by the next morning all the marks were gone as if it had never happened. As far as the paint residue left on Nathan the attendant would take a pressure washer and vigorously give Nathan a good cleaning. Even though the water was extremely cold and intense he never tried to cover himself. The residue would disappear in the drain which was located in the center of the shelter.

The drink of the day for Nathan was the same every day, one small glass of water at room temperature. The food of the day, or at least when Nathan actually got any food had a lot to be desired.

The bucket Nathan had been given to use would sometimes be cleaned and sometimes it would not. The stench lingered throughout the shelter. The only time Nathan was even allowed out of his shelter, was during the time his family would visit him. But just as soon as the family left the facility, Nathan would be taken back to the shelter. This room was so bad even rats refused to stay in there. The little light in Nathan's hole was so bad that two fire flies in heat would have given off more light.

On visiting day there was a routine to follow. Nathan would be taken to a private area that only staff members were allowed. This way no one else would ever see Nathan. Three orderlies wearing white mask would go early that morning to Nathan's shelter. Two of them carried two sharp sticks, and the other carried a spray bottle. They would remove Nathan from his room by poking him numerous times. The stench was so bad that even the mask did not help. Once Nathan was removed from his area, he was ordered to stand still. Nathan was not allowed to wear clothes while in his shelter. The third orderly would take the spray bottle and squirt soap all over Nathan's body. With the water hose they sprayed him down. The orderly always wore gloves for two reasons. One he did not want any of the stench on him. The other, the water was freezing. Once the spray down was complete, Nathan was given new clothes to wear. Nathan did not even have a blanket to sleep on in his room just a cold and clammy floor. Even the rats and bugs wanted no part of it.

Early one morning a car pulled into the mental facility where Nathan was. Three people got out of the car. It was Nathan's' parents and Angel, his sister. The nurse mumbled under her breath, "Oh crap", and paged the doctor.

He replied," I'll meet the family. Get the lunch room to fix his breakfast, so it will be there when they get to his room, and get the orderlies to clean him up and make it fast". Nathan's breakfast was being prepared, 3 scrambled eggs, toast, bacon, jelly, orange juice and a cold Dr. Pepper, along with a small cup of ice cream for being such a good little boy. The three orderlies ran to Nathan's shelter to prepare him for his visit. The closer they got to the shelter the worse the smell became. They didn't know if they would have time to get that smell off him. When they opened the bars they could not believe their eyes.

One shouted, "How is this possible?" A few moments passed, still in shock, the orderlies were not sure what to do, how could this happen? Meanwhile the doctor met Nathan's family at his second room. When Nathan's parents opened the door, they were amazed that Nathan's room was spotless, air freshener on the wall, and breakfast tray full, hot and fresh. When they asked where Nathan was, the doctor quickly said one of the nurses must have taken Nathan outside for his morning exercise in the playground.

A big smile emerged on both of Nathan's parents face. Jeff said," We'll walk out there and surprise Nathan".

At that moment the nurse paged the doctor and said to call the orderlies at once. When he did the orderlies shouted, "Nathan's gone".

The doctor said, "What do you mean he's gone?"

The orderly said, "He is not in this room". It appeared little Nathan had crawled through the doggie door and escaped.

The doctor shouted, "You better find that little **devil** and now". The orderlies split up and began searching for Nathan. Several nurses got in on the search. While the search was going on, Angel took the ice cream off of Nathan's tray and went out back to eat.

The screams and cries of a man filled the halls. Jeff asked Ruth to keep Angel in the room. He followed the doctors and nurses as they ran toward the noise. Upon entering the back dock, they were once again shocked at the scene. There was Angel crying. There stood little Nathan on the ramp totally naked and smelling to high heavens. Inside the dock a noise, like no other, could be heard. A "Crepitus noise", a medical term known as the sound of broken bones being rubbed against each other. For there in the garbage hopper was the attendant begging and reaching for help. He was flopping back and forth with blood curdling screams and cries as he was being crushed by the hopper from the feet up. No one dared to give aid for fear of being pulled into the hopper by the attendant. There was a safety switch on the platform to prevent such an accident from happening.

This was no accident. Nathan was standing on the safety switch. As the attendant was being dragged down by his feet in the crusher, he was flopping back and forth in the hopper like a fish with blood squirting from every orifice in his body. Jeff lunged for Nathan and pulled him from the safety switch, but it was too late. With a final scream for help, the attendant was gone. After the hopper crushes the material, it pushes it into a compactor. The compactor was on its way back to the ready position. One of the nurses screamed. For there on the deck of the compactor, lay one hand and one ear of the attendant.

After everything settled down, Jeff approached the Doctor. He had taken his jacket off and placed it around Nathan. He was furious and demanded to know what his son was doing naked and why he smelled the way he did. The doctor played the smell off by saying apparently Nathan had been playing in the trash that was to be placed in the compactor. Try as he might he could not come up with a viable reason as to why Nathan was naked other than to suggest he had removed his clothes and placed them in the hopper along with the attendant. Jeff told the doctor that he would not tell Ruth about this incident, this time, but that it had better not happen again. Jeff requested clean clothes and took Nathan to a room to shower and clean him up. They went to his room to spend time with Ruth and Angel.

As the family was leaving the doctor requested no more visits until further notice. They never figured out how Nathan had escaped from the shelter. Once Nathan's parents left the facility, two of the orderlies escorted Nathan back to his shelter. When they reached the bars the two orderlies ripped his clothes from his body and repeatedly punctured his skin with their sticks. Leaving dozens of marks on his white naked skin until the points of the wooden sticks were dull, covered in blood. Sometimes they would kick little Nathan in the back of the head and right above his tail bone therefore, causing Nathan's little body to go into severe nerve convulsions. The convulsions caused violent facial and head injuries from the concrete floor. The impact was so severe you could almost hear bones breaking. Nathan never cried or tried to fight back. With all the verbal and physical abuse that Nathan had received since his birth, it was no wonder he had turned extremely violent and murderous against anyone that crossed his path.

Before leaving Nathan's room, sometimes the two orderlies would urinate in his water and laugh as they were doing so. Nathan would stay here for another three months with daily visits from the orderlies and their sharpened sticks, until another facility agreed to take Nathan, but only with certain provisions.

The other facility had three patients that were considered dangerous and psychotic. To dangerous to ever be let out into public again. The facility agreed to swap Nathan for the three patients. The director of the facility gladly accepted the trade. They had no idea what they were about to receive for the three patients. This was a blessing. The day came for the trade. A police escort was brought in to facilitate the transfer due to the danger involved. First the three patients would be delivered to the facility where Nathan was incarcerated. The police escort would bring Nathan back to the new facility. When the three patients got out of the van, they were shackled and bound. The facility met them with open arms and smiles. Guards retrieved Nathan from the shelter where he had been for several months. When the staff put Nathan in the van and saw the van leave the facility, it was party time. Even the other patients were excited to see this evil child of death and destruction leave. At least the facility would once again know peace and serenity.

The facility informed Nathan's family of his new home, and they would be able to visit him in a few months. This time frame would allow the doctors to evaluate Nathan and try to help him. After the four doctors completed their individual evaluation, they met and discussed their findings. Their conclusion was that Nathan should never be let out to reap havoc on the public. As far as his extremely small size and the color of his eyes and skin they had no answer to give. The child shows no remorse, feelings, or consciousness. It is our conclusion that the child should be destroyed. If for any reason he is let out on society, rest assuredly destruction and death will follow in his footsteps. Well the time arrived, visitor's day. Nathan's family, Jeff, Ruth, and sister arrived as many times before. Ruth and Jeff visited Nathan. Angel, Nathan's sister visited him. While Angel spent time with Nathan, Ruth and Jeff met with the doctors.

The doctors simply stated his brain waves showed a very high intelligence, but he just refused to communicate or associate with the human race. After the family left, the doctor ordered that Nathan be placed in a solitary dungeon. Here he would stay until the doctor's figured out what to do with him. No one told his family Nathan was locked up 24/7. The only time Nathan was allowed outside his enclosed room was with a two man security detail while his room was being sanitized and cleaned which only consisted of 3 hours a month. Even Nathan's meals were delivered to him at his room and placed through a small flip door which was designed for that purpose only.

I believe that society refused to accept Nathan. During Nathan's 3 hours a month outside the room, he was enclosed in a steel cage 10 ft by 10 ft. which was located in the corner of the courtyard. This way he could not make physical contact with anyone else.

The main thing that freaked the staff members, patients, and visitors was his overall appearance. His skin was still as white as a snowflake and his eyes pitch black. What really concerned the other patients and visitors was this small child had two armed guards. Plus, the child was handcuffed and shackled with a muzzle over his mouth. A muzzle like you would see on a furious attack dog. This was unimaginable to visitors. Of course something like this as you might guess, was the main topic at the hair salon and the coffee shop and spread like wildfire. What added mystery and fuel to the fire was that no one knew or ever heard of this child. Every time someone asked, including reporters the final answer was I don't know or no comment. Well, months went on and rumors and gossip escalated.

Finally it was so bad that on lookers would line the fence hoping to catch a glimpse or even a picture of this freak.

The only person, it seemed, that Nathan would respond to at all was Angel, his sister. One afternoon the family had made their visit and left. The order of visit was always the same. Ruth, Jeff then Angel would visit Nathan and always one at a time. One of the doctors visited Nathan's room just like always, after a family visit which was a standard protocol. Upon entering Nathan's room the doctor stood in awe. He promptly notified the other doctors of what he had discovered. Written on the inside of Nathan's door was a poem. The poem appeared to have been written in blood. How in God's green earth could such a small child have thoughts of this caliber devastate his mind? This is what was written.

Behold these eyes
How lifeless how still
Destined for immortality
Destined to kill
Has entered this world
Through violence and abuse
From the moment of time
He's had no need for human use
He's been deemed an outcast
From all mankind
Now adopted by Satan
Vengeance he will find
His eyes shall never know no tears
He shall never feel pain
God help you for what you've created
For in hell he will reign
God can't save you for
What you have done
Welcome my friends
Meet **Satan's son.**

As soon as the other doctors saw these writings, the guards removed Nathan from the room immediately. They took photos of the room, and also took blood samples to be analyzed for content.

Finally, Nathan was returned to his room and checked for cuts and injuries. None could be found. The blood test came back positive as human blood. The source was never detected. Now for the question of the day, whose blood was it and where did it come from? After a long investigation no conclusion was ever found. They took all the information including photos and blood test and sealed them in a locked security file. They thoroughly cleaned Nathan's room of all pictures and the writings from behind the door, so that they would never be seen by anyone else.

Something like this could not be kept a secret. It didn't take long before the entire staff found out. The doctors decided if the staff found out it would not take long before the visitors would find out. It was decided to do another facility like theirs had been done. Get rid and unload this son of Satan before chaos would hit the facility. After an extensive search and due to the fact that no other facility would take Nathan, the only alternative the doctors had was to send Nathan home to his parents. The parents were called to come pick Nathan up. After arriving at the facility, the parents signed a release for transfer into their custody and Nathan left the facility to return home. Jeff and Ruth thought it best not to let anyone know about Nathan's return home, so they made sure it was night time so the neighbors would not see Nathan return home. The doctors led Jeff and Ruth to believe that Nathan was finally cured.

Chapter five

I~t seemed no matter~ what happened, there was always an incident that would break up the monotony. Here again is one of these unusual situations that will keep occurring throughout the lives of Jeff and Ruth and their children. At the local police station, the duty officer put a notice on the bulletin board that all officers should take extra care tonight, since it was Friday the 13th. A lot of crazy things can and will happen. He called everyone to sit down for roll call. There was always anxiety and anticipation during this time. Pot luck would be the officer who got stuck with the sector where Nathan lived. After roll call the drawing began. A coffee can was filled with different numbers written on wooden chips. The numbers represented each sector or coverage area within the police jurisdiction, so when an officer withdrew a wooden chip from the coffee can he knew what area he would be assigned. The only chip that officers did not want to pick was Nathan's area, chip number 13. Call it a coincidence, Nathan's address was 1313 killing lane. We won't mention what city in Alabama.

To their relief a new officer named Coy J. picked the number 13 chip for the day. He was unaware of the chaos affiliated with the number 13 chip. His first shift was going to be one he would never forget. Coy's first day on the job just so happened to be Friday the 13th and to make things worse a full moon was predicted in the forecast. All the chips were drawn and assignments were notated.

As Coy J. walked out of the room the desk sergeant replied, "Keep a constant patrol on Killing Lane". And good luck. Coy J. turned and smiled then got in his patrol car. He thought the desk sergeant was making a joke due to the street name and the date at hand. All the officers hit the street for their shift. Coy J was making his patrol when he finally got to Killing Lane. He had made it half way down the street when he looked to his right and saw what appeared to be two men arguing. He called it in and stopped.

When he got out of his patrol car, he asked, "Gentlemen, is everything ok?"

One gentleman shouted, "No, it is not".

The officer replied, "Sir what's wrong?"

The man turned with a confused look on his face. When he saw the officer, he knew right then that this was a new-be, a green horn, fresh out of the police academy. The gentleman replied, "Well buddy, I can see right now you have been suckered in". "My name is Randall. This idiot standing next to me is Jeff. He is the father of the wild child. The problem is not just me, but everyone in this community is tired of having their pets dismantled. We've had enough.

Officer Coy J. replied, "Wild child, what are you talking about?"

Randall replied, "It's Friday the 13th not that it matters with his son." With the **devil** child, everyday is Friday the 13th."

Officer Coy J. turned to the other man and said, "Ok, sit, what's going on"?

The other man said, "Officer, my name is Jeff and my son gets blamed for anything around here that happens when it comes to a negative situation.

Randall shouted, "Negative situation, my ass. Officer let me save you sometime. I just want him to keep his little **devil** on his side of the fence". When the officer looked over at Jeff, he could not help but notice a small child looking out the window.

Jeff spoke up, "Officer, sorry about this, my neighbor is highly paranoid".

The officer, still looking at the child in the window said, "Alright, not another word from either of you. Both of you go home."

Randall took about five steps towards his home then turned around and said, "Ok, have it your way, but understand this, it's early and the day is not over". Randall went back home. The officer thought it a little strange. That night was trick-r-treat. He had seen little Nathan looking out the window and thought it was a child wearing a costume. The officer cleared the scene and went back on patrol. Two hours later officer Coy J. returned to Killing Lane as part of his regular patrol. There the officer saw Randall once again standing on the sidewalk. Randall flagged the officer down and said, "I told you! What are you going to do about this?" Officer Coy J. followed Randall into his back yard. As he walked into the back yard to get a closer look and to access the situation, there was Randall's cat tied about four feet off the ground. The cat had been tied to the ladder, at least this time the cat was not dead. Randall shouted, "Well, what are you going to do?" He had to shout to vocalize his comment over the noise of the cat, crying and screaming, tied to the ladder.

Officer Coy J. said, "I'll take care of it". There stood Randall, his wife, and their three children watching the officer and the cat screaming bloody murder. When officer Coy pulled the rope the cat was free. The cat stopped crying after a loud crashing sound. Randall's children started crying and Julie, his wife, started throwing up. Randall lost it then, shouting and cussing officer Coy.

Coy called for back-up, shouting "1048-1315 Killing Lane!" Within a couple of minutes other officers arrived at the scene to assist.

Once at the scene other officers tried to calm Randall before he jumped on officer Coy. The police captain arrived at the request of the other officers. By the time the captain arrived, Julie had taken her children back inside the house. When the captain asked what happened, Officer Coy said, "I did not do it on purpose".

Randall started cussing again and said "I told you".

Coy said, "I untied the cat. I did not know it was a booby trap, so when I pulled the rope to untie the cat, it released the ladder. The cat went up and the ladder came down, decapitating the cat". The cat's body shook on the ground about a minute after the decapitation. I guess it took that long for the other eight lives to leave its body.

The captain went over to Jeff's house to confront him about what Nathan had done this time. After knocking on the door several times, it was obvious, Jeff or his family was not at home. After the captain returned to Randall's house, he told Randall that no one was home.

Randall asked, "So what are you going to do about it?"

The captain said, "Did you see Nathan do this?".

Randall replied, "No, but you know he did.

The captain replied, "Randall, I believe he did, but without proof, pictures, video, witnesses, there is nothing I can do".

Randall shouted, "What good are you, just get the hell out of my house and off my property".

So the officers left. Coy turned his report in that night. He simply put "cats cause of death, guillotine. In fine print he added that the cat ran out of nine lives. Around dinner time the next day the police got a call to respond to 1313 Killing Lane. Two officers responded to the address. Upon arriving, there stood Jeff in the driveway. The officers were wondering what type of carnage now. Jeff walked them around to the side of the house. He showed them his windows, or what was left of them. Someone had broken every window on the east side of his house.

The officers asked, "Well, do you have any idea who would do this"?

Before Jeff could say anything, Ruth said, "Yes, I do". While holding up an empty Bud Light beer bottle in the window. She said, "I noticed when we pulled up Randall was drinking a Bud Light on his front porch".

The two officers walked over to talk to Randall about the broken windows. Randall was still on his front porch drinking a beer with his neighbor Joe.

When the officers asked Randall about the broken windows, Joe stood up, "Why are you asking him".

One officer said, "Sir this does not concern you. You need to sit down and shut up".

Joe looked at the officers and said, "Listen here you little Barney Fyffe want to be I'm Mr. Randall's attorney, so I will tell you the same thing you told him yesterday. Do you have a witness, photos of him, or a video throwing the Bud Light beer bottles through the window? In other words, proof".

One officer said, "No".

Before the officer could say another word, Joe took his bottle, reached over to Randall, held it up, and tapped his bottle against Randall's, then said, "well, rent a cop want to be, Mr. Randall wants you to get the hell off his private property. You are not welcomed here."

The officers looked at each other with their mouths hung open, turned with their heads hanging down and walked off. All the while, Joe and Randall were busting out laughing.

Randall looked over at Joe and said, "Thank you. How much do I owe you?"

Joe smiled and said, "I could use another Bud Light". The officers returned to Jeff's house and told him without proof there was nothing that they could do. They then turned and left.

When they passed by Randall's house, just to make things worse, Randall shouted, "Hey", the officers stopped. When they did, Randall stood up, raised his bottle, and shouted, "This Bud's for you." They chugged them down. The officers were so mad. Their faces turned as red as a baboon's butt. They drove off. Things were out of hand.

Anytime something happened that ended in a negative moment, Nathan was the guilty party. Even if a dog, cat or even a squirrel was run over in the street, Nathan was the reason this happened. Well, four weeks had passed with no police, no fire trucks, no medics, no TV crews and no highly excited neighbors. Finally, a taste of the dull life, four weeks, this had to be a record. A taste of the dull life was much welcomed. Now, five weeks had come and gone.

On the morning of the sixth week, Jeff and Ruth woke up at the same time. They rolled over, looked at each other smiled and with tears in their eyes went back to sleep. The peace and serenity was over whelming. There was a knock at the bedroom door, Ruth said, "Yes, what is it?"

Angel replied, "Are we going to eat today?"

Ruth got up and started cooking. When she was just about done, she called Jeff, "Honey, suppers ready".

Jeff walked in the kitchen and said, "What?" Ruth pointed towards the clock.

When Jeff saw what time it was, he looked back over to Ruth. They both started laughing. Ruth shouted, "Ok kids your 1:00 pm supper, breakfast is ready." This was the most rest and relaxing time that Jeff and Ruth had seen since the birth of Angel and

Nathan eight years ago. After their one O'clock meal, Jeff went to the grocery store to get something to grill out that evening. Ruth finished the dishes while Angel and Nathan watched TV. When Jeff returned home and pulled in the driveway he called Ruth to the garage.

Upon entering the garage, she looked in the truck and said "you're joking".

Jeff said, "No honey, we've had six weeks of peace and harmony. Our luck has got to change."

While pointing at the truck seat, she replied, "Yes but what about theirs", for there in the front seat was two of the cutest little kittens you have ever seen. They were purring and meowing with excitement. The kittens had been rescued from a shelter. They immediately fell for Ruth and Jeff. Jeff called Angel and Nathan to the garage. When the two kittens saw Nathan, well it was sad and funny at the same time, both kittens bowed up and hissed at Nathan. They jumped through the rear sliding glass window of the truck backwards, hit the bed of the truck, and then scaled the side of the garage. They went through an open vent at the top of the ceiling. When Jeff walked outside, the two kittens were nowhere to be seen. Angel took Nathan's hand and walked back into the back yard to play on the swing. Jeff walked back in the garage, and there stood Ruth. He looked at her then said, "Well what", Ruth started laughing. They carried the groceries into the kitchen.

Ruth looked over at Jeff and still laughing said, "Here kitty kitty".

Jeff looked at her and started laughing as well. "Well honey", he said "it was a good idea".

She replied, "No honey, it wasn't".

"Yes it was", he said.

She started laughing again, all she had to say was "Here kitty kitty". Jeff shaking his head turned and walked off.

That evening Jeff was getting ready to grill out, when he heard Ruth calling him to come here. Jeff hurried to the garage where Ruth was standing at Jeff's truck. Pointing inside the truck she said, "Honey, you'll never guess".

Jeff shouted "I knew they would come back". Jeff rushed to the truck and looked inside.

Ruth smiled, turned around, and started walking back inside the house. While laughing, she was singing, "Meow, meow, meow, meow".

Angel came running into the garage and shouted, "Did the kittens come back",

Ruth replied, "No honey, but they did leave your Jeff a surprise in the front seat".

Angel went running to the truck and looked inside and shouted, "Pew that's gross".

Jeff just said, "It's not that bad, It's just cat droppings I guess the sight of Nathan literally scared the crap out of the kittens". Angel went running back into the house. Jeff stayed to clean up the surprise the two little kittens left it in the seat and on the back of the seat as well. Jeff started grilling while Ruth set the table.

Everything was ready, the whole family, Jeff, Ruth, Angel and Nathan sat down at the table. Ruth said, "Honey if you don't mind I would like to say grace".

Jeff said, "Sure have at it".

Ruth started," Lord bless this house and family, thank you for the bounty in which we are about to receive, amen".

Jeff said, "Amen",

Ruth spoke up and said," Oh by the way Lord, p.s. One more thing, bless those two little kittens wherever they may be". Ruth looked at Jeff, biting her lip trying not to laugh.

Angel said, "Daddy". Jeff did not reply. One more time Angel said, "Daddy".

Jeff turned and said, "What baby".

Angel said, "Here kitty kitty." Both Ruth and Jeff busted out laughing. Angel started laughing. You could almost see Nathan crack a smile, "**almost**".

They finished their meal. The kids went to their rooms while Jeff and Ruth finished the dishes, and went to the living room to watch TV. Jeff got the remote control and pressed the on button. Just as soon as the TV came on, he hit the mute button. Both Jeff and Ruth started laughing. It was a cat commercial. He turned the station, and they watched a western. The rest of the night was comical; Jeff or Ruth could not look at each other without laughing. Well, the movie's was over, and the kids were asleep. Jeff and Ruth went to bed. This time they had to sleep back to back. The thought of the two kittens would not go away.

The next morning Jeff was awakened by Ruth poking him in the ribs. He said" What", She replied," I hear a noise downstairs".

He said," I know", she replied," Well". With another poke in the ribs he got up.

Slowly, Jeff walked down the stairs. There Angel was with her knees on the couch and her arms positioned across the back head rest. Angel was looking out the window. Jeff said, "What's wrong?" Angel pointed across the street. When Jeff looked out the window, he knew their peace and serenity was over. For there across the street was a neighbor the neighbor was shaking and pointing her fingers towards Jeff's house. Also, standing next to her was a police officer. There was a knock at the door, when Jeff opened the door, there was another officer with a not so happy look on his face. Jeff just reached over signed the ticket and said" I'll clean it up". The officer turned to his partner and the neighbor and gave them the thumbs up. The officer said" thank you" then closed the door.

Jeff met Ruth in the hall and showed her a ticket for $650.00 dollars. Ruth smiled and said;" Well it was fun while it lasted". Jeff put some rubber gloves on and went across the street. With one big pull, out popped one of the kittens. One more pull and a loud suction sound, the carcass came off, but the little kitten's head stayed in place. Needless to say, internal organs of the kitten were displayed. The neighbor and one officer became very sick. It appeared that little Nathan had caught the two kittens and shoved their heads into the dual tail pipes on the neighbor's truck.

After Jeff had cleaned up the mess, he went back home. Jeff walked in and looked at Nathan. When Nathan looked up at Jeff, Jeff just said, "Morning son". He went to the bathroom to clean up. Jeff never noticed the blood on Nathan's shoes. Angel cleaned Nathan's shoes before anyone ever noticed.

As far as the rest of the day, it was the usual response. The phone calls from animal rights concerned pet owners, neighbors and a host of Nathan's admirers from the dark side. Early the next morning Jeff answered a knock at the door. A judge who had been presiding over Nathan's case had an officer deliver a summons to bring Nathan to his chambers at 4:00 pm sharp. Jeff and Ruth, along with Angel took Nathan to see the judge at 4:00 pm. When they got there, a deputy was waiting at the back door. This was prearranged with the judge. There was no need causing a scene by bringing him in the front door. Jeff and Ruth sat down with the judge. He did not have a happy look on his face. The judge said "Nathan has violated his parole". "I said no more dead animals". The two Officers are going to put him back in the mental facility".

Jeff said, "One question judge, how did you find out so fast about the two kittens?"

The judge said, "Your neighbor across the road is my sister". The judge picked up the phone and said, "Send them in". Three men in white uniforms along with three officers entered the room. After Jeff, Ruth and Angel said good bye, Nathan was taken away. Just as soon as Nathan and his escorts reached the van the deputies were not taking any chances. They handcuffed and shackled Nathan to the van's "d" rings. As an added precaution, the three orderlies took syringes and gave Nathan a shot. When one deputy asked, "What and how much?"

One orderly said," the contents are not important. But it's enough to incapacitate a fully grown man".

One deputy asked, "Is that too much for a small child"?

The orderly replied, "This is no ordinary child". After the injection, the three deputies sat in the back of the van. All three officers had their tasers pulled and ready. Two of the orderlies had two more injections ready to give Nathan. The bottom line was 6 fully grown men were terrified of a small old boy. Jeff, Ruth and Angel returned home.

Upon arrival at the mental facility, there stood the staff and patients to see the return of this little **devil**. Once Nathan entered the building one of the deputies pitched the cuff keys to an orderly. All three deputies ran to the van and left. Once inside the facility the three orderlies were met by two more orderlies carrying black jacks. They escorted Nathan back to his area once again.

When the deputies returned they informed the judge. The judge said "Well boys, its election time right around the corner, and I don't need this crap. Help me through this, and I won't forget when it comes time for promotions". The judge sent a letter to the mental facility informing the doctors not to let that little devil out. If they did and anything happened, it would be on them. They would be held responsible for any carnage that would occur.

As far as Nathan's situation, it was all negative. His lodging was not fit for any living human or animal. It was so bad that Nathan refused to go in there. But after several shots with a taser and a foot to the back of the head, Nathan was pushed in his hell hole once again. The nurses refused to go and check on Nathan while he was in the room. So Nathan's well being was left up to whatever orderly was on duty. When it was time to eat, Nathan got left over's being whatever was left on Nathan's plate that the orderly did not want. His drink was always the same, a glass of water at whatever the room temperature was. Also, Nathan was not allowed any spoon or forks. So he had to eat with his fingers and to make things worse little Nathan was placed in the room with no clothes. For whatever reason they thought Nathan would use the clothes as a weapon. On top of that, the orderlies never went to the room without their tasers and black jacks, they too were terrified of Nathan. The orderlies always seemed to have time to shock Nathan a few times. They figured if they had to tend to this animal they might as well have a little fun while they were at it. Inside the room Nathan had no water, no chairs, and no bed to sleep on, just a cold, clammy, empty room. Nathan had to sit or sleep on the damp floor.

Orderlies would bring a plastic bucket one time a day for Nathan to use the bathroom in. They would take the contents and dump them in a vented drain area just outside Nathan's room. Sometimes they would not empty the bucket for days. Remember this room was located in an abandoned part of the facility. Some of the staff did not know it even existed. It had been condemned by the health inspector many years ago.

It was rumored that Nathan would go three to four days without food or water. To give you an idea of the room conditions, once a month they would take tasers and move Nathan from his room. They took a water hose and sprayed down the inside and the floor. To see the crap and the smell was beyond belief.

There was always at least one orderly who would get sick and throw up. The room condition was so bad they would not go inside. To make things worse, they blamed little Nathan, for them having to come in early or stay late, since no one else was ordered to tend to him. Once they hosed the room they would not even take a mop and dry the floor. Before they put Nathan back in the dungeon, they would put Nathan in the corner and laugh as they took the tasers and would shock him repeatedly with force. They laughed as they would see the electrical pulse arc off his skin. For a moment the orderlies seemed to enjoy their work. They would take Nathan, put him back in his room, take an industrial high pressure water hose, squirt washing solution on him and hose him down. One orderly stuck his hand in front of the high pressure hose. He jerked it back and shouted, "Crap that hurt like hell". But it did not detour them from vigorously spraying little Nathan's naked body with the freezing high pressure water. They would really got a kick when they took the fully charged tasers and, would place them on the wet floor in Nathan's room and turn them on. You could see the electric current arcing from the wet floor into the bottom of Nathan's little feet and toes. At some point during this, you could see the veins in Nathan's pearly white legs pulsating through his skin. During all this Nathan never moved, flinched or made a sound. He just stood there. I don't care who you are. No adult could with stand this type of torture without screaming or making a sound or passing out. But Nathan just stood there and endured it all. After awhile it was no longer fun. The batteries were so weak the white and blue electrical arcs were no more. The orderlies would shut the door leaving little Nathan in this wet freezing room. No light or cloths was ever given to poor little Nathan.

This would be his life until the doctors found another facility stupid enough to take little Nathan off their hands. So began the search. In the medical field rumors travel about certain patients that stand out or have special talents. Nathan was at the top of the list. The doctors checked everywhere. Word was out. No one would take this little devil. One doctor had the solution. He had heard of a new facility that had just been built in Tennessee. All the doctors there were fresh out of school. They contacted the new facility. Doctor Ramos was head of the facility. When Dr. Ramos asked," Why the transferee", they told him "their facility was used to housing the more adult violent criminals the type that was never to be let into society again. Their sweet Nathan was just an 8 year old boy that had got lost in the shuffle some where along the way". Dr. Ramos asked to view the files on Nathan before he made a decision. They said, "no problem".

The next three days doctors and nurses prepared the paper work. There was no way they could send the original files about Nathan. These three days were spent sugar coating and making a new set of files. Man did they ever sugar coat them. The new files were sent to Doctor Ramos. After Dr. Ramos and his staff viewed the files, they were baffled as to how Nathan was ever put in that type of facility to start with. Dr. Ramos called Nathan's doctors and agreed to take little Nathan off his hands before some of the other patients incarcerated there hurt Nathan. When in real life all the staff, doctors, and inmates were terrified of Nathan.

Dr. Ramos asked, "What time can we expect Nathan?" He hardly got the sentence finished when one doctor spoke up, "We have staff members who will be in that general area tomorrow morning. They can drop off Nathan on the way". Dr. Ramos agreed. While the doctor gassed up the van three orderlies went to prepare Nathan for his transfer. They vigorously washed Nathan with the hose, and pitched him a towel and told him to dry himself off. One nurse brought Nathan a shirt, pants, underwear, socks and shoes. This was the first time Nathan had worn clothes of any kind in the 14 months he was there. Even throughout the 14 months of neglect, torture and lack of hygiene and food, Nathan strived. When the nurse walked in and saw Nathan and his pearly white naked body, she started mildly giggling. As she went from his head down, she stopped about halfway on his body. She began to laugh wildly and loudly. She made a comment about that certain part of his anatomy. The three orderlies busted our laughing. She asked one of the orderlies, "Do you have a camera, I've got to take a picture of this". Nathan just stood there naked while they had their laugh and took pictures. After they had their fun, they gave Nathan his clothes. He got dressed. They took him to the van.

The doctor said, "Are you ready?" They handcuffed Nathan and shackled him to the "d" rings in the van. The doctor left in the van with Nathan, also present with two nurses, each holding a syringe. Also, three orderlies wearing rubber gloves and each holding a fully charged cattle prod were present. The trip was fast and swift. Upon arriving at the new facility, the orderlies removed the cuffs and shackles. They put a hooded sweater over Nathan and gloves and sunglasses basically anything to cover his body.

Dr. Ramos met them at the entrance. He noticed the way Nathan had been dressed. He remembered reading in Nathan's file that he was allergic to sunlight, a new type of unknown skin disease. When Dr. Ramos signed the transferee papers, he gave a copy to Nathan's old doctor. He looked at Nathan and turned around. He replied, "What the crap". They were gone. The doctors, the two nurses, and three orderlies were nowhere to be seen. Dr. Ramos walked a few steps and opened the door. All he could see was a white blemish followed by a cloud of dust. Dr. Ramos told one of the nurses to take Nathan to a room and get him squared away. So she did. Dr. Ramos was taking another look at Nathan's file, when once again silence was broken in room 13, Nathan's new room. Dr. Ramos and other staff went running toward the sounds of screams. Upon entering room 13, they stopped. What was this thing that stood before there. Whatever it was, did not match the files given to Dr. Ramos. The staff and Dr. Ramos slowly backed up. They exited the room and locked the door. Dr. Ramos made numerous attempts to contact Nathan's old facility. Each time they hung up on him. Five days later Dr. Ramos was able to talk to Nathan's old doctor. The only thing Nathan's old doctor said was," You signed the transfer papers. He's yours. Don't ever call me again". And he hung up.

Dr. Ramos knew there wasn't but one thing to do. He called Nathan's family to come in for consultation.

Two days later Dr. Ramos received a package from Nathan's old doctor. When he opened it, he was furious. It was Nathan's original file. The cover letter showed two things. One it showed Nathan's file, revision. Item two was a big yellow smiley face and the words, have fun. Early Saturday morning, Jeff, Ruth, and Angel arrived at Nathan's new facility. They told Dr. Ramos they had not seen Nathan in over 14 months. Each one was allowed to spend time with Nathan. Jeff went first, and then Ruth had her time, Angel was last. Angel would always bring Nathan cookies or cake. Nathan wasted no time in consuming them. It was as he had not seen food in 14 months. After the visit was over, Dr. Ramos said he would re-evaluate Nathan and contact them as soon as he had a conclusion. Monday morning Dr. Ramos received a phone call from a highly excited nurse. She shouted, "You need to get here, now". When Dr. Ramos arrived she said, "You need to look inside Nathan's door". This is what he saw.

Behold these eyes
How lifeless how still
Destined for immortality
Destined to kill
You've tortured his body
But will never break his mind
When it comes my time for you
I won't be as kind
He will live forever
Not feeling cold or pain

My son will lead us all
And in hell he will reign
Take heed, "ye" mortals
Cry and scream all you can
Because it's only the beginning
When you've been touched by my hand
A warm welcome you will receive
Your time will soon come
For here I'm waiting
I'm the ruler
My name is **"Satan"**
Nathan is my son

These words appeared to be written in human blood. Without hesitation Nathan was once again removed and put in an isolated room with no human contact. The only contact was when the doctor talked to him through a small opening that consisted of steel bars. Of course Nathan never said a word. After several weeks, Dr. Ramos was getting highly excitable, and aggravated with Nathan. One morning Dr. Ramos had all he could stand. He looked at Nathan with fire in his eyes," You are my first case. I won't be made a fool of. I don't' care if there is a **devil** in **hell**. You will respond and talk to be before it's over. You have no idea who you're messing with. I will put you through so much hell and torture; you'll sing Mary had a little lamb".

So it began again, electric shock, starvation, introduced to temperature conditions and various drugs that would either throw a full grown man into full coma or kill him. Nathan endured it all. This infuriated Dr. Ramos to no end. Dr. Ramos lost his control. He took Nathan to the trauma treatment room, disrobed him and strapped him down on a table. He reached over and grabbed Nathan's gentials and pulled them up, and said. "Ok you little **devil** you have ten seconds to talk to me or I'm going to take this knife and feed it to my dogs". Dr. Ramos started counting," ten, nine, eight, seven, six, five, four, three, two, one". Still holding Nathan's gentials with his left hand Dr. Ramos started his swing with the scapel in his right hand. All of a sudden the lights went out throughout the entire facility. It was pitch dark in the majority of the rooms. Patients were screaming, and the nurses were shouting. The emergency lights came on. This still gave limited visibility. It was enough light to calm the patients and nurses down. Protocol warrants that any disruption like this merits a head count of all staff and patients. One by one the nurses started. Everyone was accounted for except Dr. Ramos and Nathan. The nurses started their search. Nathan was not in his room. Every room had been checked except for the trauma room. One nurse named Samantha opened the door. With an ear piercing scream she fainted and fell into a pool of blood. Everyone converged on the trauma room. The amount of blood dripping from the table was horrific. Nathan was still strapped to the table and was covered in blood. There was Dr. Ramos.

After clearing the scene and reading his notes, it was determined that Dr. Ramos had lost his grip on reality. He could not deal with the fact that a small child had out done him. According to Dr. Ramos notes, he was going to take Nathan apart one piece at a time starting with his genetials. Then his fingers, and toes, then if Nathan still refused to talk to him he would start with Nathan's teeth removing them one by one. Strange things happen for a reason. It was determined all three things happened at the same time. At one instance, at that one moment. When Dr. Ramos was in the process of his swing to remove a body part he stepped on a naked wire, which blew the breakers, which blew the lights, which in turn shot a electrical current causing a muscle spasm, jerking his wrist, causing a miss direction of his swing causing him to cut open his own wrist all in one perpetual movement. Dr. Ramos lay dead on the floor. He bled to death by his own hand. Now you may call this a leap of faith, you may call this a freak accident, or you may call this one touch of the devil's hand. Even the death of Dr. Ramos could not shake the thought of the nurses seeing Nathan's pearly white body laid out on the table. For censored reasons, the jokes will have to remain better not mentioned, as far as Nathan was concerned, call it bad luck. But poor Nathan wound up in another dungeon. At least this one did have a light. One more time doctors decided to transfer Nathan to another facility, no matter what it took, so the search began.

One evening as Jeff and his family sat down at the dinner table for supper, they were discussing their day and how well things were going. This was a rare moment. Ruth started telling them about her day the restaurant. The crowd seemed to be larger than normal and they also seemed hungrier than usual. Even to the point she had to order extra supplies from the local vendor. Her photo shop called. A couple wanted to book her for their wedding pictures. The problem was there was a lack of attire; the couple wanted the pictures taken in their "birthday suits". After a long discussion, Ruth resolved the issue, Bathing suits and a free dinner at her restaurant.

Jeff began with his day. He was telling about how one of his workers, named Glen, was handling wooden pallets when he was bitten by a large brown recluse spider.

Glen shouted, "I've been bit", at first everyone thought he had been hit with a fallen object. When they ran to give him aid, they realized what was going on.

One supervisor said, "You sit down, and I'll get the truck and take you to the hospital". When he went to sit down he jumped up and screamed. Out of his mouth came words that cannot even be put down on paper. Let's just say he had a colorful vocabulary.

One worker replied, "Dang I bet that hurt".

Glen had sat on a large nail that was protruding out of the wooden pallet. "No replied the old man".

"Then why the scream and all the colorful words," the supervisor asked.

Glen raised his other hand. He had been bitten by another large brown recluse spider. The supervisor rushed the man to the hospital.

Ruth asked, "So how is he doing?" Before Jeff could answer, there was a knock at the door. When he opened the door, there were three police officers and two detectives. The detectives entered the house.

Their first comment was, "We need to see Nathan".

Jeff replied, "No you cannot".

The detective said, "I wasn't asking, I'm telling you, I want to see Nathan and now". Ruth walked in the living room where Jeff and the officers were talking.

Ruth replied, "What's happened now".

Before Jeff could say anything, one officer replied, "We want to see Nathan and your husband said no. So we're taking him down town for further questioning. I'll tell you Mrs. Ruth, I want to see Nathan and now.

When Ruth said, "No you can't", you could see the veins pop out on the forehead of the detective. As far as the other detective, he was as red as a baboons butt. Another officer spoke up and said, "Looks like you're going downtown also". As officers took Jeff, Ruth and Angel downtown, other officers searched and searched the house for Nathan.

Back at the police station, Jeff, Ruth and Angel sat in the interrogation room. When the chief walked in you could tell he was not a happy camper. He yelled," This time that little devil has gone too far, I have reports of missing animals in my hand", and with that comment, he threw them on the desk. The chief shouted, "Are you so stupid, you don't think I can figure this out. In case you forgot, I live on the street behind you. This time things have gone too far. Now my little girl's two kittens are missing, and if that's not enough, my brand new German Sheppard puppy is missing. He was supposed to be our next police K-9. You refused to answer my officers, so let me tell you now, I'm the chief and you will answer me or sit here in this jail until you're old and your teeth fall out. Now for the last time, where in the hell is Nathan?"

At that moment the door opened, a voice spoke, "That's it, you're done, it's time to go".

The chief replied, "Oh hell no".

The voice at the door was Jeff's lawyer. After a reminder from the lawyer of all the code violations his officers broke back at the house, like entering without permission or a search warrant and several others. H even mentioned a lawsuit, and that was it. The lawyer left the police station followed by Jeff and his family.

When the officers returned to the station without Nathan, the butt chewing began. The chief had the same problem as one of his officers, the veins on his forehead were popping out. Jeff and his family returned home followed by their lawyer. They were going to discuss the actions of the police, and if Jeff and Ruth wanted to pursue any legal actions against the police department.

Ruth came back into the living room and said rather loud, "Yes, I want to send them a bill for $200.00".

The lawyer asked why, "Ruth replied, "Those darn fools ate all of the supper I had fixed".

The lawyer planned on sending the police department a catering Bill for $500.

The lawyer looked over at Ruth and said, "So Ruth, how is Nathan doing".

She replied, "He is still in the mental hospital and has been there since you took him there five weeks ago. We would have told the officers that if they would have given us the chance, but they all acted like a bunch of boneheads". The lawyer told Jeff it's a good thing you have me on speed dial.

Ruth replied yes, I hit it as we were being escorted out the door. The missing animals still remains a mystery to this day. The lawyer and Jeff and his family never told the officers that Nathan was in the mental hospital, or was he? If Nathan didn't do this, then who did?

The next day, Jeff received a very disappointing phone call. He called his wife and told her the contents of the call. He told her he was going to take the rest of the day off. He was going to go play golf with his good friend Bruce. Feeling Jeff's disappointment, she left work early. Ruth decided to fix Jeff a really fantastic dinner. When Ruth got home, she had her game on. She marinated two large rib-eye steaks with Creole spices, sautéed mushrooms, and fixed a large salad with spicy ranch dressing and topped that off with a three gallon jug of sweet tea. To make the dinner special, she lit several vanilla candles and had soft music playing. Ruth being a very attractive lady didn't hold back. She wore her Harley motorcycle leather out-fit to enhance the evening. All these things added up. When Jeff got home, there was a bubble bath waiting on him. We won't go into details, but Ruth accomplished everything she had set out to do, and then some.

Remember Glen, the man who was bitten twice by two brown recluse spiders, he died. That was only part of the phone call that Jeff had received. The man's wife, June, had gone into the kitchen two days prior to his death. While cooking dinner, she burned her hand on a skillet. It was a minor burn, one you would classify as "first degree". The next morning June got up and screamed. A noticeable amount of blood was on the bed. She was holding her hand. Her finger looked like she had a case of severe leprosy.

Her husband rushed her to the hospital. The nurses filled her with IV's and antibiotics. After numerous test and blood work the nurses wrapped her finger and sent her home. June said she was not in any pain so no pain medication was prescribed. That night the antibiotics and meds seemed to be working. Glen and June went on to bed.

The next morning Glen was awakened by another scream. This time June's entire hand was swollen. The smell of rotten flesh was over whelming. Once again Glen rushed her to the emergency room. Again the same IV's and test were given. After hours and numerous tests in the emergency room they finally figured out that they had no idea what was going on, or what to do. This time they put her in the hospital. Glen went home that night to take care of the house and clean up the mess in the bedroom. The next morning when Glen returned to the hospital to see his wife, he was stopped at her room entrance by a security guard. When Glen asked what was going on the security guard said, "Sir, this room has been quarantined. Absolutely no one allowed inside."

Glen asked, "Why, What's going on."

The security guard said, "Sir, I haven't been told anything other than no one goes in." At that moment June's door opened. The only thing Glen could see was a large piece of plastic. A nurse came out of the room wearing a full hazmat suit. Glen became very agitated, demanding answers and to see his wife. After some very colorful words the doctor came out of the room wearing the same type of clothes as the nurse. He told Glen to follow him down to his office where they could talk in private. Upon entering the doctor's office, Glen saw three other gentlemen sitting there. The doctor introduced Glen to the three other gentlemen. They were from the center of disease control (CDC). They began to ask Glen dozens of questions. When was the last time he was out of the country, did he bring back anything, did he have visitors or receive anything from another country. They wanted to take blood samples from him. When, one of the three men noticed the two bandages on each hand of Glen, he told them he had been bitten twice by a large brown spider. The look on their faces showed they did not believe him. He went ahead and agreed to give blood. Numerous times Glen asked about his wife. No answer was given, just question after question by the three CDC officers.

Finally Glen stood up and shouted, "That's enough!" No more questions until you tell me what's going on and what's wrong with June.

One of the CDC officers asked, "Who's June".

Glen replied, "My wife. She is in the room where the security guard is, you idiot".

Another CDC officer said, "Why enough, have you got something to hide. At that point Glen got up and started towards the door.

One CDC officer asked, "Where are you going, we're not done". Glen never said a word. When Glen reached to open the door two police officers appeared. The CDC officer shook his head "no" while looking at the police officers.

One officer spoke up and said. "Sir, when they say you can go, then you can go, but until then you are not allowed in that room". The other officer told Glen to go back and sit down in the chair and not cause any problems. Glen turned around, went back and sat down in the chair. When the CDC officers started asking more questions, he just sat there.

Glen finally spoke up and said, "I'm done answering questions. It will be over my dead body before I answer anything else. I want to know about my wife and now. I'm done with your bureaucratic BS."

One CDC officer said, "Well Mr. Glen, that may very well be the case".

The doctor said, "That's enough, I'm taking him to see his wife".

One CDC officer said, "Okay, but only on two conditions, one he wears the suit and two he cannot touch his wife". Glen agreed. Glen put the suit on and went down the hall to his wife's room.

The doctor looked at him and said, "I hope you're ready". Glen went inside. When he pulled back the curtain to see his wife, he stood there in awe. That thing on the bed was not his wife.

She opened her eyes and spoke, "Honey, it's ok". It was June or what was left of her. Her arms were bandaged up to her shoulders. Her ears and nose were gone. Her face was nothing like he had ever seen before. With tears in his eyes he reached to touch her left hand which was badly disfigured. When he touched her left index finger she moaned, due to the intense pain. She started crying.

Glen moaned, "Oh God honey".

The doctor shouted, "You were told not to touch her. Now see what you've done". The doctor reached down in the floor and picked up June's finger off the floor. No blood showed from her hand where the finger came from. But the horrific smell was unbearable. It was the smell of rotten flesh. The doctor took Glen back outside.

Glen asked, "What the HELL is wrong? What's happening?"

The doctor said, "we don't know. I have never seen anything like this before. The fact is your wife is falling apart, literally, one piece at a time, and we don't know why".

Glen asked, "Will she be ok? Will she be able to walk out of here?"

The doctor said, "I take it you didn't notice her feet are gone". Glen fell back in the chair. The doctor told Glen that was the reason the CDC officers were here, to try to help. Glen went to the waiting room. He could not comprehend the devastating condition of his wife.

Now you can call this ironic, fate, or just weird, but two hours later the doctor went to the waiting room to tell Glen the findings of the CDC officers. The doctor said, "Mr. Glen, the CDC officers have finally settled on a diagnosis. Your wife has contracted a rare disease caused by an infection when she burned her hand on the skillet. The disease is called "*__man-eater disease__*". I'm also sorry to tell you that your wife has expired". The doctor dropped his head and began to cry. Glen did not hear him, because he had died as well. June had died from the man eater disease and Glen had died from complications of being bitten twice by the large brown recluse spiders. The doctor determined that Glen and June's time of death was exactly the same time.

Now you know what the phone call to Jeff was about. To this day no one has stepped foot back in

Glen and June's house. There are rumors that family members of Glen and June want the land, but as far as the disposition of the house, they have all agreed on one thing, **burn it,** so they did. The disposition of the land is still in court. At the grave site, there was only one casket. A regular full size casket for Glen. June was buried with Glen in the same casket. Glen was buried in his favorite suit. June, on the other hand, the man eater disease had done its task. Due to the devastating condition of June's body, there was only one way the coroner could collect her remains. One of which he had never done. The corner gathered up her remains with a heavy duty vacuum cleaner. He left her remains in the bag with a tag, written on the tag, remains of June do not open, highly contaminated. That's how they were buried together. The coroner took the vacuum cleaner and burned it as a safety precaution to ensure no one else would be contaminated from the left over residue inside the vacuum cleaner.

Jeff and Ruth would have gone to the burial at the grave site if they had known. At least there would have been two people there to pay their respects. The bottom line was Glen and June's family were too afraid of catching what June had contracted. So life goes on.

Oh, by the way, usually coroners are supposed to have a strong fortitude and to not show emotions. If you can get the coroner to talk about it, he will tell you that never will he do that again. For he will tell you between the horrific odor of rotting flesh and the sound of body remains being sucked up in the vacuum cleaner, it is not a moment that will soon be forgotten.

He was one frog hair from passing out. I know the coroner who took care of Glen and June was my uncle. He resigned shortly after that. It affected his mind so bad that for months and months, just the sound or even the sight of a vacuum cleaner would cause him to throw up and become very sick. So I guess, the next time you see a coroner get out with a vacuum cleaner; take my advice; **RUN**.

Now let's go back to little Nathan. After an extensive search, they found another facility that would take Nathan. When the new facility asked why they wanted to get rid of Nathan, the doctors sent a fax. It simply stated. Our facility handles only adults and most of these are considered too violent for society. Poor little Nathan was a small child that they acquired because he had no other place to go. They were worried that some of the other patients might hurt or even kill little Nathan, when in fact the Staff and other Patients were terrified shitless of Nathan. A few day's later arrangements were made for Nathan's transfer. They told the doctors at the new facility where Nathan would be sent they would deliver Nathan to them since they had other business to conduct in that area. When Nathan was leaving the facility, he turned and looked back and just like before. The staff and patients stood there at the windows and doors cheering and laughing. Finally, this little devil was no longer part of their lives. Right before Nathan was at his new facility, the doctors removed the handcuffs and muzzle from Nathan. They did this so the new facility could not see what they were about to receive at their door. When the Doctors introduced Nathan to his new doctors, he just stood there not saying a word as usual. The new doctors were told that Nathan's appearance was due to a rare skin disease. And the reason he did not speak was that he was real shy. The fact was Nathan's doctors had never heard him say a word from day one. The transfer was made and a copy of Nathan's file was given to the new doctors. The fact was for the last two weeks the doctors had spent their time making up a new set of files. They did not dare let the doctors see the real files. I don't know how fast the van that had transported Nathan was ever driven, but, on this day when they left Nathan at the new Facility, I'm sure a new record was broken, and you could hear the Doctors laughing from inside the van as they sped out of sight.

Chapter six

Nathan's new doctors decided to give Nathan two weeks before they started their analysis. This would give him time to settle in. And then they could start a new file on Nathan. Nathan's parents had been notified of Nathan's new home and were told to wait three months before their first visit. This way the doctors could evaluate Nathan and give them the results. It did not take long before the doctors noticed that the files that they were given did not match what they had been given by the other doctors. They decided to contact the former doctors and request the proper files on Nathan. They faxed the former doctors numerous times but to no avail. After several attempts by phone, they finally contacted one of the doctors by phone. The phone call was short and direct. The former doctor's voice was concerned. He said, the files that were given to you were our own interpretation of Nathan. You can draw your own conclusion. He's your problem now. Don't ever contact us again. Deal with it". Numerous visits were made by three different doctors. Their findings were basically the same. They had been lied to by the other doctors about this little child called Nathan. Their conclusion was that they had never seen a child like this before.

This child showed no response or feelings, or anything that could be considered human like. This child seemed to be possessed by another force. Through other test like electrical impulse and scans, his IQ was pretty much off the charts. He was brilliant. It was determined that with his intelligence that if Nathan ever met the dark side, that chaos and mayhem would surely follow his foot steps. He should never be let out on the public. The safest thing to do with this **devil** would be destroy him, "simply kill him".

These three doctors became enraged by how they had been lied to by the other facility and staff. The doctors contacted Nathan's old facility. No one would take their call. Two weeks later a certified package was delivered to Nathan's new doctors. It was from Nathan's old doctors. On the outside of the package, was a big smiley face and a note have a nice day. The package was Nathan's real files containing all of his records including the ones that were sealed in a vault. After looking at these files, the doctors became even more furious. When the doctors received Nathan's new files, it was like pouring salt on a wound for what they had done by tricking the new facility into taking Nathan. Well, the doctors decided after reading Nathan's real files to make the worst of a no win situation. It was decided to keep all the files together, including the one that they started plus the ones that were kept from them from the other facility. Until, they could figure out what to do with Nathan.

One of the main concerns was that this facility was housed for children only. The deal was that Nathan had been rejected. He was considered to be **too** violent for an adult facility. The law suits and legal ramifications that could follow them if something were to happen would be too devastating. To try to keep such a thing from happening and to cover their butts, the doctors once again moved Nathan to an isolated area that had been forgotten about where he would have no contact with anyone except for a selected few. He was kept in this room twenty four hours a day and seven days a week.

The only time Nathan was even allowed out of his room was for one hour a week which ocurred during the cleaning of his room. He was under security where he was chained to a post in an area and very early in the morning when no other patients or visitors were up and walking around. Months went by with numerous visits by the doctors to no avail. The only time there seemed to be any change in Nathan's activity was when the family would visit, which was once every two months. To keep their butts out of trouble, the doctors had told Nathan's family that there would be scheduled visits only. This way the doctors would have time to take Nathan out of his dungeon and put him in a nice room for the family visit. Once the visit was over and the family left. Nathan would be returned to his isolated room. This again would be Nathan's life until the doctors could figure what to do with him. The routine was always the same during the family visit first Ruth then Jeff then Angel, his sister. According to Ruth and Jeff, Nathan never acknowledged them at all. It seemed that Angel was the only one who could communicate with Nathan. The doctors believed it might be because both of them were considered to have such a high I Q or even some type of mental telepathy. But none of this could be proven. It was just all speculation.

After every visit from the family, the doctors would visit Nathan's room. There they would find drawings that were so detailed and precise, to a tea. It was unbelievable that a child so young could possess such talent. The drawings could be matched to the staff without hesitation. The one thing that would under normal circumstances freak out the staff was the drawings of graphic and gothic nature of torture to animals and some people in Nathan's drawings. But they were talking about this child that was destined to cause pain and death if he was ever let out into the public. The drawings were more detailed and could have not been more exact if you had taken them with a photo.

During one weekend visit the doctors and staff thought it would be a good idea for the children to have a special visit while they were all out in the courtyard. Their surprise was the doctors had contacted numerous pet stores and agreed to have dogs brought to the facility for a community Day. In the past this was always a big success with the children and families. In the process homes were found for some of the pets. All the families were out in the courtyard with the exception of Nathan and his family when all of a sudden several trucks pulled up at the gate. As the trucks pulled inside the gate, you could tell that the dogs and children could sense something, and that a great day was about to take place. The dogs and children could feel the presence of each other, or so it would seem. The dogs were barking and jumping, and the children were shouting and clapping. Needless to say, there was a stampede when the doors of the trucks opened. Every dog knew exactly what child to go to, and every child knew instantly what dog or puppy was theirs. A couple of hours had passed. Everyone was having a blast. Once again the idea was a big success.

One of the handlers asked the doctor if all the children had a pet. Was there any child in the facility that had been forgotten about? Before the doctor had time to think, he said yes one child. This child was a special case, and the doctor advised against having Nathan participate. While trying to explain that it would not be a good idea at all, the handler said he had two Animals, one puppy and one dog. he had saved for a special child. After a brief discussion the doctor reluctantly agreed to let the handler take one pet to Nathan's room. The handler said these two pets were guaranteed to make any child laugh. The doctor laughed, "Not this child they won't".

The doctor told Nathan's mom and Jeff of the idea, and they liked it. Mom and Jeff waited outside Nathan's room for the little puppy. Angel waited inside the room with Nathan. The handler started walking down the hall with the cutest little puppy, waging his tail like a car's wind shield wiper on high speed. Surely Nathan would respond to this little puppy. About ten feet from Nathan's room the dog stopped and locked all four legs on the floor, when the handler pulled at the rope, the puppy began to cry and howl. When the handler picked up the little puppy and took two more steps towards Nathan's room, the little puppy pissed all over the handler. The handler said the little dog must have gotten sick so he took him back to the truck. He returned with the bigger dog which was just as cute as the little puppy. Again when the handler got ten foot from Nathan's room, the dog locked all fours on the floor. When the handler pulled at the rope, the dog growled at the handler and started crying just like the little puppy. The handler said he had never seen the two dogs act like this. He was really shocked that the bigger dog growled at him. This was the first time the dog had shown any aggression what so ever. From the room Angel hand in hand with Nathan entered the hall. Without thinking the handler saw Nathan and said "holy shit" when Angel took Nathan's hand and pointed towards the dog. The dog curled up in a ball and tried crawling away. The dog messed all over the floor. Poor little Nathan and His sister just stood there looking. The dog acted like he had been shot or something worse.

The handler shook his head and said. "Doctor, you're crazy, I'm not taking my dog nowhere near that freak". He turned around and took the dog back to the truck. The further away the dog got from Nathan the more calm he became. Angel took Nathan by the hand and went back into the room. Nathan's parents stood there crying.

The doctor told Nathan's parent "I'm very sorry. We have never had this happen before".

Nathan's parents responded, "That's ok we have seen this happen, and more than once". You know they say that animals can sense danger and evil when it's near. But of course that's, just more speculation and has never been proven by the science world".

The end of the day had arrived. The whole day was a big success with the animals with the exception of Nathan's experience.

Things went back to normal, for the next eight weeks. On the next visit by Nathan's parents, Nathan had been left out in the courtyard with his sister. With all the visitors and patients, Nathan had been forgotten about and left in the back courtyard. Nathan had been left out there while his room was being cleaned. Take note. None of the patients or their families had ever seen Nathan since he had been put in an abandon part of the facility that was no longer in use, or at least everyone had thought. The thing was that when these family visits occurred, Nathan was always brought back to a part of the facility that was in use. His family never knew of his regular room where the doctors had him incarcerated. It was one of these things that was better left not said, or brought to anybody's attention. Great preparations were made to assure that no one ever saw Nathan during his stay at the facility. It was working pretty well. While the doctors met with Nathan's family, Angel was with Nathan out in the courtyard. Due to the confusion the doctors thought Nathan was in his room.

A tragic oversight. All of a sudden ear piercing screams and cries broke the morning silence. Staff, visitors, and patients converged to the back courtyard. As children entered the courtyard with their parents, they began to cry and started throwing up. The carnage was one of disbelief. It was something you might expect to see in a Steven King or Alfred Hitchcock movie. For there, covered in blood and guts facing towards with his arms extended and palms facing up was Nathan with blood dripping from his fingers and pooling on the ground. There stood Angel crying in shock. The carnage was what was hanging from the clothes line above Nathan's head. There on the clothes line was what was left of the four beloved pet **cats** that belonged to the facility. The pets were no more. All nine lives could be seen leaving their hides. It seemed that Nathan had taken all four pets, tied their tails together, and threw them over the clothes line just to watch them claw and bite each other until all nine lives left their skins, Nathan took duct tape and wrapped it around the cats just so their guts would stay in longer, and the carnage would last for several minutes longer than normal. Or whatever normal is in this manner, and it did. They were dead. They died in a manner that could not be forgotten.

After the initial shock, someone finally said, "Where in the **hell** did this freak come from and who did he belong to?" At the same time some of the parents were escorting their children back into the facility to get them away from this unthinkable act. No one knew what to do. They just stood there in a state of awe. Again, "Who does this thing belong to with anger in their voice"? Nathan's parents just stood there staring with the rest of the people and never said a word. When Nathan started walking towards his parents, they were terrified and turned and walked away. They did not want anyone to know Nathan was their son. All of a sudden the sound of sirens echoed through the grounds. Someone had called 911 requesting police to the scene. When the officers entered the courtyard, they just stood there looking.

Someone shouted, "Get that freak out of here now." The officers slowly approached Nathan and grabbed him by the arms trying not to get blood and guts on their uniforms and took him inside. They put plastic sheets in the patrol car and cuffed Nathan and took him away. Even the officers were scared of Nathan. It took a while to clean up the carnage. It's hard to imagine that four little cats could hold so much blood and guts. Oh yes, let's don't forget about all the discharge from the visitors and patients who could not stomach the scene.

When the families found out that Nathan had been living there among their children, well, all hell broke loose. Phone calls from the media and attorneys representing the families stormed the facility. When the officers arrived at the station, they put Nathan in a holding cell. The entire station was shocked. What was this thing and where did it come from?

Two officers took Nathan down stairs to another holding cell. He would have to be cleaned up. He was covered in dried cat blood and guts. The problem was that no one would get close enough to clean him up. One of the officers took a high pressure fire hose and sprayed Nathan from outside the cell. After being sprayed, the officers told Nathan to sit there, and they would be back later. They left Nathan there in the cell dripping in wet clothes and still not cleaned from the earlier event. The doctor called the police department and told the chief not to bring that little devil back to his facility. After five days no one knew what to do with this child. On the sixth day a police car arrived at the facility. Two officers got out with Nathan in handcuffs. They gave him back to the doctor and said good luck. He is your problem. Don't call us again with anything pertaining to this child.

After five more weeks they could not find anyone to take this child. So they did the one thing that they could do. They called Nathan's parents and asked them to come to the facility immediately. When they pulled up at the facility and got out of their car, they were met by the three Doctors, with Nathan right behind them.

They simply said, "Here he is. Take him home and don't bring him back. Don't call us ever. He is yours".

By this time the family had moved to another area, made new friends and found new jobs. The friends and neighbors did not know Nathan even existed. When they moved into the new neighborhood, they took what few photos they had of them and Nathan and placed them in the attic. They told Angel never to talk about her brother to anyone for any reason. Their family had already disowned them because of Nathan. As far as their friends and neighbors knew, all of their family was dead and Angel was an only child. When a couple of the women asked why only one child, she told them about the attack which left her unable to have any more children. The parents knew that one day someone would find out about Nathan, and their life would be in shambles. So again, why worry about something you can't control.

More than once they had talked about moving and changing their names. Home life would be so much easier. But the simple fact was, Nathan was their son, and they had not reached that point "yet". Early one morning the parents woke up and looked outside. They were amazed at the beautiful sunshine and how it glistened off the dew of the green grass. They decided it would be a good day for a picnic. Well, due to their special situation with Nathan, the only choice for a picnic was in the back yard. The parents worked hard and fast at setting up a mini-beach. You could not ask for a better scenic view. The birds were singing, and the squirrels jumping from limb to limb. They went upstairs and woke up Nathan and Angel and said, "We have a surprise for you. We're going to have a Picnic". Angel jumped out of the bed with eagerness and joy. Nathan just got up with no emotion as usual. When the parents took Angel and Nathan outside, the birds and squirrels left. Well, I guess, Mother Nature got pissed for the parents messing up the day for the animals. Because within a few minutes, a dark cloud appeared over the horizon and with it came the rain. The parents were forced to take the picnic inside. They set up inside the breeze-way just inside the house where they could enjoy the cool breeze and the mist of the rain outside.

About half way through the picnic, they heard a strange noise. When they turned around, there were three stray cats, wanting in looking for relief from the rain. When the cats saw Nathan, they bowed up and took off running. One cat ran outside. The other cats ran in the house and upstairs. Ruth and Jeff made an extensive search but, the cats could not be found. They finished the picnic and enjoyed the rest of the day playing board games. Ruth and Jeff could never win. It seemed the intelligence of their two children was well beyond theirs.

Three days later Jeff was outside working in the yard. While the children were upstairs playing in their rooms and while Ruth was watching TV. She kept hearing a strange noise. She finally turned the TV on mute. The noise was coming from behind the couch. When she pulled the couch away from the wall, there it was. She ran outside grabbed Jeff and said, "Help". When he said, "What"? She told him to go look behind the couch. He did and backed up clinching his teeth. He went to the kitchen and got a trash bag. He slowly walked back into the living room with a pair of rubber gloves and a stiff swallow. There behind the couch were the two cats from the picnic. Both had an electrical cord attached to their fur. The electricity was still hot. It appeared that Nathan had hooked the cats up to the live wire and fried them. The sound that Ruth heard was the electricity pulsating through the cats. The other sound was one of the cats was still barely alive. But that soon passed.

As far as a description of the scene, let's just say they had a bad hair day, and leave it at that. Jeff took the cats and wire and placed them in the trash bag. He took them to a nearby creek and away they went. When he returned to the house, both parents just looked at each other. Some things are better left unsaid.

So time went on. One week had passed, and everything was good. So good that Ruth decided she was having a craving for some fresh (catfish), so while she stayed at the house with Angel and Nathan, Jeff took off at the crack of daylight. He remembered a honey hole from when he was a small boy. Back then it had some really good catfish. Now, they should be good eating size. About noon Jeff pulled in the driveway, Ruth watched to see if he had any luck for the Day. To her surprise he had fifteen large fish in the back of the truck. Yes, they were big catfish. They averaged four to ten pounds each. While Jeff cleaned the fish and prepared them for cooking, Ruth ran to the store where she gathered all the trimmings. She was ready with french fries, tarter sauce, ketchup, and the ingredients to make home made hushpuppies, and sweet tea. Angel and Nathan stayed in the back yard playing. When Ruth returned from the store Jeff had just finished cleaning the last catfish. While Jeff cooked the fish, Ruth fixed the trimmings. Angel was watching TV, and Nathan was in the back yard playing in the sandbox. Ruth set the table and went outside to help Jeff with the fish. When Ruth returned to the kitchen, she saw Nathan and Angel checking out the trimmings that were prepared on the table.

She told the children dinner would be ready in about twenty minutes. So Nathan went to watch TV. Angel went outside to play on the swing. About Twenty five minutes later, Ruth shouted, "Time to eat." Man, everything looked fantastic and smelled twice as good. They fixed their plates and dug in for dinner.

"Darn it's good" Jeff said. Ruth noticed Angel had her plate full except for one item. But, she did nothing. Thinking that Angel had all she wanted in her plate. Angel seemed to make a strange face every time Ruth and Jeff would take a bit of the one item.

Jeff noticed and said, "Take your time. There's plenty to go around". Angel just shook her head. Ruth did notice a few extra tid-bits of meat in one item. She thought Jeff had added an extra surprise to the fixings. Dinner was a success. Everything was consumed. After dinner Ruth and Jeff complemented each other on a fine dinner as they washed the dishes and cleaned the table.

Nathan went outside with Angel to the sandbox. As she approached the sandbox, she noticed something sticking out of the sand. She moved some of the sand back to see what it was. When she saw what it was, she stood up and looked at Nathan and said, "Nathan how could you do this"? Nathan just stood there looking at the sandbox. Angel said," I'm not going to tell mom or dad". They could not deal with this". She sent Nathan back in the house. She went and got a shovel and buried what was left. It appeared Nathan had cut up what he could and put it in with the fixings. The family ended the night watching movies and eating pop-corn. Angel never said a word about what she had found in the sandbox.

The neighbors never found their two little puppies. I guess that's the reason they call them hush puppies. They are dead and can't bark. So for the next several days, once again, all was well. Until, late one afternoon Angel came running in, grabbed Jeff and pointed to the back yard. When Jeff ran out into the backyard he found Nathan by the fence. On the other side of the fence were three of their neighbors taunting Nathan. Jeff had recently reported them for bullying and harassing Nathan. When Jeff shouted at them, they said, "Ok, were leaving". They may have been the neighbor-hood bullies but these three were still scarred shitless of Nathan. Ruth and Angel stood there looking from the kitchen with tears in their eyes. Jeff called a meeting. All four sat at the table. He simply told Nathan and Angel sometimes people are mean to each other. That is the way life is.

Ruth said, "And yes, someday those bastards will get theirs". Nathan turned and looked at his mother and but never said a word.

Three days went by. All of a sudden the morning silence was broken by the sound of sirens. "What now", shouted Jeff. The sirens stopped up the street at one of the neighbor's house who had been taunting Nathan. A tragic accident someone said. He had been working on his car breaks. When the jack gave away, his head was split into when the hub fell on his face. This was ruled as a freak accident. One of the other bullies went to his friend's house to tell him of the accident. After three or four rings of the door bell, there was no answer. He heard a noise out back; the faint sound of music. His friend was out back. When he rounded the corner into the back yard, he couldn't believe his eyes. It looked like his friend had fallen from a ladder impaling him-self on four wrought iron post. One post protruded clean through his pelvic region, one through his chest, his neck, and the other through his mouth. And there on the end of the fourth post were his false teeth. This was also ruled a freak accident. After the 911 call, the third bully, for some unknown reason, packed everything up and moved that afternoon. I guess he did not want to stay around and wait for another freak accident to happen to him like it did his two friends.

Two days later Ruth and Jeff were working in the back yard when a loud scream came from inside the house. Ruth and Jeff stopped, looked at each other, and went back to work. A few seconds later another loud scream came from inside the house. Once again they stopped working. Ruth said, "Ok, go see what's wrong".

Jeff said, "Why".

Ruth said, "You're the man of the house, so go".

Jeff said, "Not today, honey".

Ruth gave him that look and said, "Go, I can't handle any more blood or carnage today. So go". So slowly Jeff walked up to the house. Just about the time he reached for the door, another loud scream came from inside the house. He turned and looked at Ruth. She pointed to say go on in. She hung her head. Slowly Jeff walked into the living room where he had found the cats. Well, there it was. He slowly turned not to make a noise. When Jeff went back outside and stepped off the porch, Ruth saw something she had never seen before. Jeff was crying. For Jeff to cry it had to be very bad.

Her first words were, "Oh my God, who and how many?" He slowly walked back to the flower garden. When he reached the flower garden he fell to his knees.

Ruth kneeled down beside him, took one hand in hers, and with the other on his shoulder. She said, "Don't worry. It will be ok. We have survived everything else. We'll make it through this". With a lump in her throat she said, "Ok, I think I'm ready. How bad is it"?

Jeff looked up and told her. With astonishment she said, "What, are you sure?"

He said, "Yes honey, a cartoon on TV". Both fell back on the flowers laughing. The rest of the day was peaceful and joyous.

Chapter seven

FINALLY THE DAY OF school had arrived. It was a new year. When Nathan walked into the principal's office, everyone stopped. The principal, Mrs. Cooley, had been a principal for 30 years, but had never seen anything like this. What was this child that was about to enter her school. His eyes were black, as if you were looking in a deep dark hole. Ms. Hardister, was called to the office. Mrs. Cooley informed her that she had two new students. When she turned and saw Nathan, she just stood there looking at his eyes. When Nathan looked up at her, she took about four steps backwards, and gasped. Being that Angel and Nathan were twins they were placed in the same class room together. Mrs. Cooley asked Jeff and Ruth to wait in her office until they had time to talk. When she walked out of the office, she told Ms. Hardister to give her weekly update on the two children. Ms. Hardister took Angel's hand and told Nathan to follow them to the class room. Upon entry to the class room, the other children started laughing out of control. Ms. Hardister tried to get the children under control while hiding the smirk on her face behind her hand. Little Nathan just stood there making no sound. His sister walked up and took his hand and sat him down at a desk next to hers.

The rest of the day the children made giggling noises and faces at Nathan. Ms Hardister would intervene occasionally, but for the most part, allowed it to happen. Occasionally she would let a comment slip out about the little black eyed creep that was among them. The children would burst out laughing, except for Nathan's sister. This went on for weeks and the more it went on the worse the taunting got and the faster news traveled throughout the school. Before you knew it, it was hard to conduct a class, because everyone wanted to see this black eyed boy with skin as white as a blanket of snow. This went on for weeks.

One morning, while Mrs. Cooley was headed to the library for a meeting she heard a commotion coming from Ms. Hardister's classroom. She looked through the glass in the door first, to see what was going on. Ms. Hardister was nowhere in sight. A few of the boys were running around the room playing tag, which is probably what the noise that caught her attention. Some of the children were crying. Mrs. Cooley stepped into the classroom and asked, "What is going on?" One of the little girls she had seen crying pointed to Mrs. Hardister's desk. When Mrs. Cooley took a few steps toward the front of the room, she saw Ms. Hardister lying on the floor unconscious. Her water glass lay on the floor beside her. She was rushed to the emergency room where they tried to revive her. But nothing they tried worked. She died. An autopsy was run. The cause of death was ruled as a heart attack.

The next morning a substitute teacher was called in to take Ms. Hardister's place. When the substitute teacher saw Nathan, he couldn't believe his eyes. He was no different than Ms. Hardister. When it came to stopping the name calling from the kids, he was actually worse. He never even tried to stop them. He would go so far as to look the other way when they were on the play-ground. As long as there were no cuts or bruises left on Nathan, the word was "anything goes". The substitute teacher soon became a favorite of some of the kids.

A few weeks had passed since Ms. Hardister had died. On this particular Tuesday, the police were called to the school. Seven children had suddenly become sick after eating lunch. They were all taken to the hospital. After a full examination and blood work was completed, it was determined that all seven children had traces of cyanide poisoning. The school was placed in lock-down mode. The lunch room was closed; food was quarantined. The police started looking for suspects. They did comprehensive background checks on all the teachers, lunchroom staff and janitors. Everyone came back clean. The lunchroom was sterilized and the school was re-opened. The police had no suspects. Someone mentioned Nathan, the weird little boy with the black eyes. The police were shocked at the sight of Nathan. One of them was overheard commenting that he looked like he had risen from the dead. During the extensive interviews with the teachers and children they found out about all the bullying and taunting that Nathan had received. With no other suspects, they decided to look at Nathan. A search warrant was requested and received for Nathan's house.

During the search of Nathan's room they found rat poison in the corner of his closet. They also found an unusual plant that no one had ever seen before. A few days after the school had been re-opened the police were called to the school again. This time there were two bodies. The substitute teacher and an assistant Football coach. Nathan was removed from the school until further investigation could be done. The news media was having a field day with this story. Within a few minutes of the broadcast, calls were coming in to the police department with information relating to Nathan. Neighbors couldn't talk fast enough. The school was a circus. There were so many reporters and on lookers trying to get a look at the bodies, that the school decided to suspend classes for two days.

The police made arrangements to have the bodies at night and transported to the morgue where the autopsies and numerous tests were to be conducted. After the autopsies were completed the coroner gave a news conference. Both toxicology reports came back clean. The coroner could find nothing unusual. It appeared that both young men had suffered a heart attack. The bodies were released and funerals were planned for both of the teachers. During this time Nathan had been charged with poisoning his classmates and was in court. During the trial, the district attorney brought up the families past and all the events that transpired, especially those pertaining to Nathan, including all the times he had been placed in the mental hospitals. The DA considered the icing on the cake all the reports and incidents involving the cats and missing animals. The DA provided pictures of some of those cases. He instructed Nathan to look at the jury. He knew that the simple eye to eye contact would help the case considerably.

During the trial Jeff and Ruth repeatedly asked Nathan's lawyer to object or say something in Nathan's defense. The lawyer would look at Jeff and Ruth and say, "Don't worry. I've got this under control". The other evidence the DA introduced was the plant that was found alongside the rat poison. One of the teachers that had been called to testify motioned for the bailiff. After a brief conversation, the bailiff got the attention of the DA and informed him that the teacher had some important Information to tell him pertaining to the case at hand. The district Attorney asked the judge for a fifteen minute recess, which was granted.

The teacher was taken to a conference room to meet with the DA. After introductions, the DA asked the teacher what information he had. The teacher asked the DA, "Do you not know what that plant is?".

The DA replied, "No, do you?"

The teacher replied," Yes, it is a plant called **Brucine.** A very deadly plant."

The DA asked, "How do you know this and why is it so deadly?"

The teacher replied, "My hobby is Horticulture, the study of plants". He began to explain in great detail. Brucine is related to strychnine. When the juices are squeezed from the plant it is a very nasty poison. A person consuming over 2 mg of pure brucine orally will almost certainly suffer. It will give the appearance of a full blown heart attack. The DA was astonished and reminded the teacher that three of his fellow teachers had died recently from sudden heart attacks, but the toxicology reports had come back clear. The teacher replied that this type of poison would not show up in a toxicology screen. You would have to look at the blood work and skin cells for that specific poison, and know what you're looking for to even detect the chemical Brucine. After recess was over, the DA asked the Judge if he could approach the bench. Permission was granted. The DA and the court appointed lawyer for Nathan walked to the bench. After hearing the information, the judge asked the teacher to approach the bench and asked him some more questions. The court appointed lawyer never objected or anything. Nathan might as well not of even had a lawyer. Not one word did he say the entire time of the trial. The judge ordered the teachers bodies exhumed.

Nathan was placed into a level one hospital ward while the additional testing was performed, to see if this poison could be found. After two weeks, they were ready to begin the trial again. The DA requested permission to present the new toxicology reports. Again, Nathan's lawyer never said a word. The test concluded that indeed a large amount of Brucine was found in each of the deceased teachers system. The closing arguments were one sided. The DA presented a full blown case of evil. He even produced the birth certificate where Nathan's name spelled Satan backwards or read backwards when held up to a mirror. The DA was precise and direct and to the point. His verdict was guilty, cold and calculated. Now, Nathan's court appointed attorney's time was at hand. His entire speech lasted five seconds. The only thing he had to say was, "My client is not guilty". He thanked the jury and sat down.

The outcome for Nathan at this time was pretty bleak. The jury deliberated for one hour and ten minutes. When the jury was reseated the judge asked the foreman, "Have you reached a verdict?"

The Foreman said, "Yes". The Bailiff handed the verdict to the judge. Once the judge looked at the verdict, he handed it back to the bailiff, who returned it to the jury foremen.

The Judge asked the foremen, "In regards to Nathan, how say you".

"**Guilty,** on seven counts of poisoning. And, **guilty,** on three counts of pre-mediated murder". The courtroom cheered, except for Nathan's parents and sister. The judge ordered two psychiatrist to evaluate the status of the Nathan and report to her directly. At which time she would give his sentence. After one month both psychiatrist had come to the same conclusion. Nathan was a "Psycho", just pure evil. After hearing the report the judge once again ordered Nathan placed in a mental facility.

The family received nothing but hardship from their neighbors. Not one person offered any type of support or friendship. Once again the conversation about moving came up, but after a lengthy discussion they decided moving to another state would not be a solution to this problem. The fees from the trial had all but depleted their savings and starting a new business in another state would be costly. After Nathan was admitted, they were allowed to visit him. The new doctors talked in length about how it would be in Nathan's best interest if they limited them to quarterly visits. This would give them time to evaluate Nathan and find the best treatment possible for him. They promised to send monthly reports to them keeping them informed of Nathan's condition. The first report was all negative. New doctors were brought in to study Nathan. After their observation and test, they provided his parents with a new progress report. This time, there was something positive to report. One doctor reported that the reason Nathan could not talk was because his larynx had not developed at the rate of the rest of his body. His larynx was so small his voice was unable to construct the necessary air. The doctors got together and told the parents that as soon as they could come up with a solution that they would call them. A few weeks went by, and Nathan's parents received a phone call. One of the doctors said that Nathan had showed remarkable progress. So remarkable that he had a surprise for them. He asked if they could schedule a good time for a visit with Nathan. They were so excited to finally be getting good news that they told the doctors they could be there that weekend. Upon arrival at the hospital the doctor welcomed them in. Being kind hearted and the fact that Nathan had made considerable progress he decided to grant Nathan a week pass. He decided that since Christmas was next week he thought the family time would be a great help in Nathan's full recovery. Unfortunately, the events that took place that week would be his downfall and Nathan would never get a pass again. It seemed as if the nurses could not get Nathan ready to leave the facility fast enough. While leaving the facility, Ruth noticed the staff at the windows and doors. They were clapping and smiling, as if they were happy to see Nathan leave.

Since no knew they were bringing Nathan home, they thought it best to take their time returning. When they arrived at home it was very late. Early the next morning the door bell rang. When Jeff opened the door, there stood a young girl about Angel's age. She introduced herself as Misty, and said they had just moved next door. Her mother had fixed her a picnic to keep her occupied while they unpacked. She was wondering if he had some kids that she could play with. Apparently the other neighbors had not met them or given them the details of what had happened. Jeff went upstairs and asked Angel if she would like to meet their new neighbor and have a picnic. Angel missed not having any friends so she excitedly ran down the stairs to meet Misty. While Angel went to the picnic Nathan stayed in his room watching TV. Angel never mentioned her brother to Misty. The entire day while Angel was gone, Nathan stayed in his room. Nothing Jeff or Ruth could say would get Nathan to leave his room. It seemed that Angel was the only person that Nathan wanted to associate with. When Angel returned home that evening, she went upstairs to Nathan's room where she surprised him with numerous treats that she had brought back from the picnic. He ate them so fast Ruth was afraid he would get strangled. It was as if he had never been given treats while in the facility. Angel actually had to get a wash cloth to clean him up. That night was one of the best nights that they could ever remember having as a family. They popped more corn and watched movies till bed time.

The next morning, while Ruth was making breakfast she heard the door bell ring. Jeff yelled he would get it. When he answered the door, it was the Misty, from next door. She wanted to see Angel. Thinking Nathan was still asleep, Jeff told her where Angels room was and to go on up. She went upstairs to Angel's bedroom but could not find her. When she came back downstairs she was told that Angel might be in the back yard playing. Misty headed out the backdoor to find Angel. A few seconds later she come running back inside. She was crying and shouting, "There's a weird looking kid out there with black eyes". Misty was so afraid of Nathan that she went home. When her parents asked her why she was back so early, she told them about Nathan, and what she had seen. They had their doubts. They brushed her exaggeration aside due to a scary movie she had seen the night before and let it go at that.

Three months had passed since the trial, and Nathan had been granted a week pass for Christmas. It seemed for the most part things were settling down. No neighbors were complaining. No police had been called to their house. According to the local weather station, there was a big snow storm brewing that was scheduled to hit on Christmas Eve, give or take a day. Neighbors were putting up decorations. The ladies of each household were exchanging recipes for new dinner menus, except for Ruth. Because of Nathan's trial the whole family had been ex-communicated from the rest of the neighborhood. Even when

Ruth or Jeff saw any of their neighbors at the local grocery store, they were given the cold shoulder. Some neighbors would even turn around and go back another direction if they met one of them coming down the aisle. They never had a problem checking out because everyone always insisted they go to the head of the line. The owner loved to see them coming to his store. He noticed that the longer Jeff or Ruth stayed in the store, the longer other people would shop just to avoid any contact with them.

Well sure enough, believe it or not, the weather men actually got it right. Christmas Eve, 4 inches of snow drifts were found in some of the local areas.

That morning Jeff and Ruth decided to let the children sleep in. They sat down to the first peaceful breakfast in awhile. Even the food and coffee had a better taste. After breakfast was done, Jeff and Ruth sat down on the couch to watch the Christmas Parade on TV. Jeff glanced at the clock and noticed it was 8:00 am. Somewhere around twelve o'clock Jeff and Ruth woke up. Everything had been so peaceful and quiet that they had fallen asleep. After a few minutes, they noticed that they had not heard the children moving around upstairs. This could not be good. Both of them slowly and reluctantly walked up stairs wondering what kind of mayhem they would encounter. They checked on Angel first, slowly opening her bedroom door. All was good; there she was covered up head to toe. Next, they went to check on little man Nathan. They slowly opened Nathan's bedroom door. What a relief. Nathan was also in bed covered head to toe. Jeff noticed Nathan's window slightly open. The cold air would not be good for him he told Ruth. As he approached the window, he stepped on one of Nathan's toys. Before he had time to think, he said a bad word rather loud. Jeff was still barefoot. The little plastic toy had pierced the bottom of his foot.

Ruth reached over and said, "I'll count to four and pull it out".

Jeff said "ok". She didn't count, not even to one. Ruth reached over and yanked the toy out. With tears in his eyes, and blood dripping from the bottom of his foot Jeff uttered another bad word. When he looked over at Ruth as if he was going to say something, Ruth simply smiled and said, "Honey, love hurts".

After a funny looking grimace came across his face, she turned and looked towards Nathan's bed. With all the noise that Jeff was making, Nathan never moved or woke up. She reached over to pull the covers back to check on Nathan. When she did, she gasped. This was not good; there in Nathan's bed, under the covers, were two pillows. Nathan was nowhere to be found in his room. Jeff forgot about his foot. Sometimes Nathan would actually go to Angel's room and lay on a quilt on the floor next to Angel's bed and sleep. They quickly returned to Angel's room. Slowly opening the door, they walked in to check to see if Nathan was there. When they looked besides Angel's bed, they looked up at each other. Nathan was not there, neither was Angel. Pillows had been placed in her bed as well.

Now was the time to get worried. They did a frantic search of the house, room by room. Jeff had placed dead bolt on the doors, but high enough up to where neither Angel nor Nathan could reach it and open the door. So once more, Jeff and Ruth did a frantic search for the two children. They finally made their way to the utility room. Jeff looked over at Ruth and asked, "What are you doing?"

"This is not good", she said. "I did not do any laundry this morning".

When Jeff opened the dryer door the odor was horrific. Both were scared to look inside. "Well," Jeff said "some ones got to stand up and be an adult about this and look inside the dryer", so Ruth did. When she looked inside the dryer, she screamed and passed out. Jeff caught her just before she hit the floor. He picked her up, carried her to the couch, and lay her down on it. He went to the bathroom and got a wet wash cloth to wash her face with. Jeff sat on the coffee table to take care of his wife. He was in no hurry to get back to the utility room. After several minutes had passed, Ruth opened her eyes and began crying profusely. When Jeff asked her if she was ok, she pointed towards the utility room. When Jeff asked her what was in the dryer, Ruth pointed once again towards the room, and threw up on the couch. Reluctantly Jeff walked back towards the utility room. The closer he got to the dryer, the worse the odor of a burnt body was. When Jeff looked inside the dryer, he was not prepared for what he found. He began crying, and then he also threw up all over the laundry room. He closed the lid to the dryer and went back and sat down by Ruth on the couch. Several minutes passed. All they could do was look at each other.

Ruth asked," What do we do, call the police or what?"

Jeff said, "No, we need to find Nathan. We need to find out how or why he would do this to a member of our family". Jeff looked over at a window going to the front porch. On the base of the window was a small trail of blood leading to the outside. When Jeff went outside he followed the blood trail. When he got to the corner of the porch, he saw Nathan. Jeff yelled, "Nathan, what the hell have you done?" Nathan turned around and extended his arms out with his palms facing up. Blood was dripping off his hands and fingers. There on the ground where Nathan stood, the ground was saturated with blood. The neighbors heard Jeff's scream and called the police. The police were already patrolling in the area. Upon arriving at the scene, the officers pulled in the driveway. Even before they got out of the car, they noticed Jeff standing on the porch, and then they saw Nathan standing in a pool of blood. These two officers were not strangers to the family. They had been called to this address on numerous occasions involving Nathan's strange situations.

Both officers put their rubber gloves on. One officer grabbed his camera and started taking pictures. The other officer escorted Jeff back inside. After taking the necessary pictures, he brought Nathan back inside. By this time the street had started to fill up with neighbors. As he was bringing Nathan inside he noticed the strong odor coming from the back of the house. As one officer took their statements, the other officer followed the odor. After entering the utility room, he looked inside the dryer and shouted "Oh my god". The other officer dropped his pad and with his gun drawn ran to the aid of his partner. When he reached the utility room and saw what was inside the dryer, he immediately threw up. He was not prepared for this. The other officer grabbed the remains and placed them in a garbage bag. At that point he took the remains in the bag and carried them to the waiting ambulance that had responded to the 911 call. The neighbors saw him remove the bag with blood dripping from it. They started counting their children to make sure they were all there. The officer returned inside to aid his sick partner and discuss the scene.

As they sat down in the living room, one officer said, "I don't know what action to take. I will have to inform our chief and the judge". At that point they heard a noise coming from the basement. One officer tried to quietly open the door, only to find it locked. After unlocking the door he cautiously opened it. There he was, face to face was Angel. She asked her mom and dad if they had seen her pet dog Spike. She had been looking for him everywhere. Jeff and Ruth had acquired the pet dog for Angel while Nathan was in the mental facility, hoping to ease her loneliness. They did not have the heart to tell her that Nathan had tortured and killed her dog. One officer told them we will contact you after Christmas to let you know what we're going to do.

When the officers walked back outside one of the neighbors shouted, "Who did that little devil Nathan kill this time?" One of the officers spoke up and said, "It was a false alarm". The officers told the neighbors that the dog had been chewing on Christmas lights and was electrocuted. The crowd dispersed. The officers told the ambulance driver to drop the bag in the river on the way back to the hospital. The rest of the day was quiet. Not much to be said, alot of looks and tears. The only positive point was the next day was Christmas. The officers told the neighbors that Nathan was still in the mental hospital under the judge's orders.

The new neighbors decided that since the next morning was Christmas they would take breakfast over to Jeff and Ruth's house and let Misty and Angel spend Christmas morning opening gifts. Early Christmas morning they did just that. They fixed a large breakfast, gathered their gifts and knocked on the door. Jeff and Ruth were surprised, but after seeing the look on Angel's face, welcomed them in. Nathan was still upstairs. During breakfast Nathan stayed in his room. After breakfast Angel and Misty ran into the living room to open presents. Suddenly a horrific scream came from the living room. All four parents went running. They were not prepared for the scene that lay before them. There stood the two little girls crying. At the base of the tree was Nathan covered in blood. On the top of the tree, well, I guess you know. There in the very top of the Christmas tree, where the star is normally placed, was the head of Misty's pet cat. The eyes were missing. So shining through the two holes, where the eyes once were was a beam of light from the Christmas lights. Hanging from the branches was the skin, legs, tail and other parts that we won't mention. Also, there was a considerable amount of blood dropping from the tree onto the presents. It took several moments of had seen for the shock to hit them, but when it did. Misty's father shouted, "What the hell is that?" Numerous words were exchanged, such that their voices could be heard a full block down the street. Not knowing what was going on, the neighbors started arriving at the house. One of them called 911. The police arrived and entered the house with a few neighbors slipping in behind them. They were not prepared for the carnage. Everyone started talking at once. "Who let him out?" "Why was he released" "How long has he been here?" Well, needless to say, the chief was called, who in turn called the judge.

The next day Jeff and Ruth were visited by the Police and DA. Nathan's family had to pay five hundred dollars for the slaughter of the neighbor's family pet. This time word spread like through the community, and even the animal rights people got involved. The whole area was in an uproar. The family was shunned, and treated as outcasts. The few friends Angel had made disappeared. How dare they turn something loose like Nathan in their community?

Luckily Ruth's restaurant was two counties away where no one knew her as the mother of the devil child. At the restaurant she could hear customers talking about Nathan and what they would do if anything like that happened in their town. She never acknowledged the fact that she even knew Nathan much less that he was her son. Ruth always arrived before anyone else. The only child anyone ever saw was Angel, and that was only on rare occasions. She had a TV and a bathroom in her office, where Angel played, which she always kept locked. If anyone ever found out, it would be the end of her restaurant. Currently, the restaurant was flourishing beyond anyone's expectations. During lunch people were lined up at the door waiting for her to open, just to beat the crowd. At night for supper it was pretty much standing room only. Now if you want to see chaos, once every two weeks she would advertise a special meal "soup a-la-carte". She would never tell what the special soup of the day was. On those days it was total chaos with standing room only. As many as fifty people would be standing outside waiting to get in. The phone would ring constantly from people wanting to know how long the line was and people wanting to make reservations. Soup day was the only day reservations were not taken or allowed. Even the mayor and his staff had to wait in line. Remember, her restaurant was in a different city than she lived in. She would always make it a point to see who was there to eat and who was coming in. She knew she couldn't take a chance on one of her neighbors walking in and seeing her.

Several of the homeless people would show up at the back door for food. She had Jeff build a separate area just for them to eat. She never charged the homeless to eat. She had them put the word out that they could come on soup day and eat for free. In return for her generosity the homeless would come back the day after soup day and do a complete professional clean up of the back area.

Ruth had three problems on soup day. One, people wanted to make reservations, even offering extra money to get them. When they were told no, they acted as if they were a little mad, but they always showed up and stood in line anyway. Problem two was she always worried about cooking enough or having enough to cook or running out of soup, which never happened. The third and probably one of the biggest was it seemed this 8:00 pm closing time, would turn into midnight breakfast. People would keep showing up to eat, and she didn't have the heart to tell them no. It got so bad on soup day that at least on four separate occasions the police had to break up a fight. As silly as that may sound, anyone arguing over soup. The good thing was it seemed every time a fight would break out at least one officer was already there whether he was on duty or off duty. You would think a uniformed officer at the scene would detour some people from causing a scene. On soup day, it was not the case. In fact some people standing in line would actually encourage such behavior. This way they could get a table sooner, especially if someone ahead of them in line was arrested for fighting. It was so bad that the day after soup day she would close. This gave her and her employees time to recover from the madness.

The next soup day just happened to land a couple of days after Christmas, so Ruth had to bring Angel and Nathan to work with her. They arrived at the restaurant very early. She knew it was going to be one of those days. To add fuel to the fire, she noticed a sign showing a county baseball tournament was to be held that day. It wasn't long before the phone started ringing. People were asking if they had started to serve breakfast. The entire time she had been open she had never served breakfast. The phone calls were constant and continuous. She had to call someone in early just to answer the phone. She was preparing for dinner. One of the employees said, "What time is the delivery truck going to be here?" Ruth glanced at her watch and realized that the delivery was late. She received the dreaded phone call. The delivery truck had been involved in a wreck, and there was no telling how long it would be before the delivery could be made. She thought she might have enough food to handle the normal crowd, but not the stampede of extras coming in. There was only one thing to do. She called Jeff and informed him of the situation. Without hesitation, he locked his office up and left to give his wife assistance. The game plan was simple. Jeff would come get a list from Ruth of everything she needed. He would go to the grocery store and purchase the items.

About five minutes later Ruth received another phone call. This time it was from one of the officers who was a regular at her restaurant. He was at the wreck with her delivery truck. When he found out the destination of the truck, he knew her dilemma. He told her to come over to the scene and he would help her load whatever she needed. She tried calling Jeff but to no avail. Being stressed and excited about the officer's phone call, she left in a hurry. She forgot about Angel and Nathan being left in her office. She arrived at the wreck to find the road closed to all traffic except for emergency vehicles. Now she was stuck in traffic for no telling how long, and on top of that she had no signal on her cell phone.

One of the officers conducting the road block recognized her vehicle, walked up to her car, and escorted her through the road block straight to the wreck. One officer offered the assistance of several men at the scene to load Ruth's vehicle with food. Now she had another problem. Her car would not hold what she needed. "No problem," one officer said. "There are no injuries in the wreck. We'll load the rest of the supplies in the ambulance here at the scene". By this time traffic was a lost cause.

Ruth said, "With this traffic at a stand-still, I'll never get out of here".

The medic said, "Hey Ruth, we have lights and sirens on the ambulance".

She replied, "I don't want anyone to get in trouble."

Another voice off in the background said, "Ruth, you won't get in trouble. The ambulance will lead, you will follow them, and I will follow you". When she turned around to see who it was, she was shocked; it was the chief of police. He was known to be a bit of a jerk; a stickler for abiding by the book only.

Ruth didn't take time to think about it. The ambulance pulled out, followed by Ruth, then the chief of police, with lights and sirens blaring. It didn't take near as long to get back to the restaurant as it did to get to the scene. When they arrived back at the restaurant with lights and sirens still blasting, Ruth's employees came running out to see what was wrong. They stood there in awe when they realized what was going on. Jeff pulled up behind Ruth as she got out of her car. Ruth turned to speak to Jeff when something on the corner of the dock caught her eye. "Oh my God", she gasped when she saw Angel. She realized in her haste to leave, she had left Angel and Nathan at the restaurant, in her office unlocked. She grabbed Jeff's arm and whispered to him what she had done and told him to find Nathan. After the food was unloaded, she turned to the medic and said, "Thank you". She turned to the chief of police and said, "Thank you too sir".

The chief said, "Hey, not so fast". He handed her a piece of paper.

She asked, "What is this?"

He replied, "Your speeding ticket". It looked like Ruth was fixing to burst into tears. The chief started laughing. He said, "Gotcha. I was just kidding. I know I've got a reputation for being a jerk."

When with a slight grin Ruth replied, "Chief I've never heard that".

The chief replied, "Just remember that when I come in this afternoon to eat". The chief got in his car and left.

Ruth got her employees organized and went looking for Jeff. They sat down and started talking and realized that the children had been left by themselves, other than the employees at the restaurant, for just a little over an hour. It was a miracle that none of her employees had seen them. How lucky can you get?

Normally during the preparations of the soup, Ruth would do a little taste testing, but this time she sat in her office, still stressed from the previous events of the day. Jeff took Angel and Nathan back home. Ruth decided to close her door for a few minutes and try to collect herself and calm down. She flipped her sound machine to the rain setting and closed her eyes for a few minutes. This always helped her relax. Unfortunately it relaxed her too much. She fell asleep in her office. Ruth was awakened by the sound of voices. She looked at her watch, "Holy crap," she yelled. Lunch was served at noon and dinner started at 5:00 pm. Her watch showed 6:15 pm.

When she walked into the restaurant she was amazed. Total chaos met her, worse than she had ever witnessed. Four people looked up at her and gave her thumbs up. They were the medic, two officers from the wreck and the chief of police. She looked at her head waitress and said, "I see the chief made it in".

The waitress replied, "This is his third time here since lunch". Numerous people stopped Ruth and raved about the soup. It was better than ever, just a little more kick than normal.

When a couple asked her what she had done differently, she simply said, "I can't say". When in fact, she couldn't because, she had not done anything different. The next morning one of the homeless people was cleaning up behind the restaurant. He noticed something unusual in the corner, placed as if it had been hidden on purpose.

When he pulled the cover back, there lay 13 dead cats. One was missing a head. Their insides had been removed. Their ribs and rear section were scrapped clean of any meat. Their bodies had been drained of all blood or any other liquids that might be found inside a live cat. The homeless man picked up the 13 dead cats and carried them back to his camp site.

Later that night, Jeff came out of Nathan's room carrying a small black garbage bag. When Ruth asked what was in it, he simply opened it up so she could see. When she looked inside the bag, she grabbed her mouth and went running to the bathroom. Jeff went ahead and took the cats head and buried it in the back yard. So now we know where the head went from the cat found at the restaurant. The homeless man was the only one to ever figure out what the extra ingredients in the soup were that gave it that extra kick. He was not about to say anything and mess up his free meal, cat soup or not. To him it was just a little extra meat in the soup.

When the judge was informed of Nathan's trip home, she had not been a happy camper. She informed the hospital that Nathan was not to be released again without her written consent. She would receive quarterly updates along with the parents. Her goal was to keep Nathan in the hospital until he turned nineteen years old. At that time, a comprehensive evaluation would be performed. This would give her the necessary information she needed to make a decision on his future. She would decide whether or not to send him home or to prison.

After Nathan had been in the hospital six months the doctor contacted the judge and convinced her to let Nathan go home for a few days. The doctor had complied with the request about sending her quarterly reports. Based on those reports, she reluctantly agreed since there had been no negative incidents at the hospital involving Nathan. Nathan's family was contacted.

Well it had been a long hard winter. Jeff, Ruth and Angel were having a severe case of cabin fever. Jeff came home from work one afternoon and said I have two surprises. First, we were awarded the contract for the relocation of the old county cemetery and the manufacturing of the water treatment plant. Second, we are taking some time off. Our businesses can do without us for a few days. Ruth reminded him there was no place they could go and take Angel and Nathan without people looking at Nathan and freaking out. Jeff said, "Honey, I have a surprise. I bought several acres of land in the mountains". Right in the middle of the land is a log home with one way in, one way out, and with a heavy duty security gate.

He told her as an additional safeguard, he had put everything in her maiden name. This way it would be very unlikely anyone would be able to track them down. Jeff explained the game plan to Ruth. They would have everything packed and ready, get up early in the morning, finish their yard work and then hit the road for vacation. While Ruth finished packing, Jeff decided to go ahead and pick Nathan up from the facility. They packed a lot of clothes and gear. They even packed their utility trailer.

Early the next morning, Jeff and Ruth were in the front yard raking leaves. Angel and Nathan were in the backyard playing. When Jeff reached to open the gate to the back yard, a blur passed between his feet. When he turned around to see what it was, it was gone. Ruth looked at Jeff and started laughing. Jeff started laughing. Jeff said, "Well, look at the positive point, no blood or carnage this time".

Ruth said, "You think you can catch it?"

"Not a chance," Jeff replied, "By now its three counties over". Jeff went on into the back yard. There stood Angel looking at Nathan. Nathan was standing there with a rope in one hand and a bag in the other. Jeff walked over and told Nathan to give the rope and empty bag to him. Nathan did as asked. Jeff turned still trying not to laugh in front of Nathan. He went back around to the front yard and showed Ruth.

She tried not to, but began to laugh, she said, "Well, honey, at least it lived up to its name". Jeff started laughing until Ruth reminded him of the fresh cat droppings on his shoe. She began to laugh even more at the expression on Jeff's face. Anyway, somehow Nathan had caught a cat, took one end of the rope and tied it to the cat's tail. He took the other end and tied it to a bag of wild rice. The crackling sound of the wild rice was enough. I guess it caused the cat to lock his paws in four wheel drive because when Jeff opened the gate the movement was on and the cat was gone. They both looked at each other and burst out laughing. Jeff went to the back yard to get the kids, while Ruth ran upstairs to get the last of their clothes; it was time to hit the road for vacation. When they pulled out of the driveway and down the street the neighbor's phones started ringing. Good news travels fast. A small celebration took place in the street. The neighbors thought they were moving.

Jeff stopped at a local store and bought a lot of food, dishes, etc. for their stay in the log home. When the cashier asked Jeff where he was going he just said, "South on vacation". One customer standing about ten foot away overheard the conservation. The customer also lived on the same street as Jeff and Ruth. When the customer got home, he noticed several people laughing and cutting up on the sidewalk, among the party goers was his wife. She came running to tell him the good news. The celebration was short lived when he told her the truth.

During their ride to the cabin, Jeff started telling Ruth about a new contract that he had acquired. Part of the contract included removing a family grave yard which was on a specific parcel of land that the government wanted. But, the owner did not want to sell his property.

Ruth asked, "Why did he sell it"? Jeff said the government wanted to build some type of government housing. When the old gentleman refused to sell it, they stole it. The local sheriff came to physically remove the old men from his property. When the old man refused and pulled a gun on the deputies, well they shot him and called it self-defense. A check was finally sent to his next of kin.

Ruth asked, "Who was his next of kin?"

Jeff replied, "We were never told who it was". He went on to explain the main reason for moving the graves in the first place was the land had been acquired through a process called "eminent domain". This is basically a legal way for the state or a government to steal land that someone does not want to sell in the first place. The land in question was also being used for some other purpose, but we were told it was none of our business. They went on with their discussion and finally made it to the log home.

Now, just to let you know, investigators found out later the check for the land went to a gentleman named Ray C, the former employee of Jeff's company. Could this be one of those small world coincidences. Ray C visited the site two months later and found the construction in full force. His uncle's house had already been bull dozed down and burned. Ray blamed Jeff's construction company for the death of his uncle and the land being stolen from the family. He still believed that Jeff had it in for him for no reason. As he was leaving the job site he shouted at some of the workers, "You think this is funny. You haven't heard the last of me. Remember "payback is hell". The workers never figured out who the man was or why he was mad at them.

It took about three hours for Jeff and his family to arrive at the front gate. As a precaution, Jeff closed the gate behind him and locked it making sure that no one was following them. Jeff, Ruth and the children made it to their log home. Angel jumped out of the truck hollering and screaming for joy. Ruth shouted, "Hush, we don't need any police here".

Jeff said, "It's ok, let her have at it. The nearest house is five miles away. The gate is locked, and there is only one way in and one way out". Jeff had failed to mention to Ruth that they had a boathouse 500 yards away on the lake.

After unloading the truck and trailer, Jeff and Ruth sat on the front porch enjoying the peace and serenity while watching Angel and Nathan riding their bicycles in the front yard. Jeff stood up and let out a scream and scared the dickens out of Ruth. She said, "What's wrong?"

"Nothing", he replied, "I'm just happy, how about you, kids?" Angel had a smile on her face from ear to ear. You could almost see a smile on Nathan's face, at least almost. That afternoon they enjoyed the evening sunset, while making good use of the grill on the outdoor patio. Jeff went all out, with rib eye steaks, boneless ribs, baked potatoes, salad and sweet tea. Jeff did notice one thing. On his previous visits to the area there was always an abundance of animals, birds, squirrels, even a few deer. Jeff dared not say anything. He did not want to ruin the moment. While Ruth finished the dishes, Jeff cranked up the popcorn machine and turned on the TV for Angel and Nathan to watch movies. It was one of the best days and nights that they could remember. Don't get them wrong. The birth of their two children was special somewhat, even that had a downside. As Ruth was finishing cleaning up the kitchen, Jeff walked up behind her and gave her a gentle hug around her waist. Ruth leaned into him and exhaled with a sigh of relief. At that moment all was well. Jeff took Ruth's hand in his and escorted her outside to the swing on the back porch of the cabin. There they sat for awhile. Ruth looked over at Jeff still holding his hand and said, "Listen".

Jeff replied, "What".

Ruth said, "I can't believe it. We've been here for almost 10 hours with no police cars, no fire trucks, no ambulances just the sound of a couple of owls, birds, squirrels, and coyote's off in the distance. Usually the only sound of animals that we ever get to hear is one of torture, and blood curling screams while their running from Nathan".

Jeff called the children outside to enjoy Mother Nature at her finest. When Angel opened the back door of the cabin, there was Nathan with her. Just as soon as Nathan stepped on the back porch, well, everything changed. It was the sound of silence. Not one sound of any animal could be heard anywhere. It was as if someone had hit the mute button on a TV remote control. The only sound was the slight sound of the breeze from the wind as it echoed off the leaves throughout the woods. When the wind stopped, it gave Jeff and Ruth an uneasy feeling. It was so quiet on the back porch that they could hear each other's heart beating. Other than that it was a "dead silence".

There are some noises that are so loud that it will hurt your ears to listen. In this case it was so quiet that it felt like someone was pushing your ear drums further inside your head. Have you ever tried to hear the sound of nothing? Think about it, it hurts. After a couple of minutes, Angel took Nathan back inside to watch more TV. Within ten minutes Mother Nature gave the all clear, and the animals began breaking the sound of silence. Jeff looked over at Ruth. Words were not needed; the look in their eyes was enough. Once again, life was good. Ruth rested her head against Jeff's shoulder, and they continued to enjoy the sounds of the evening.

Ruth started, feeling something warm on her face. She gently squeezed Jeff's hand. He looked over at her, and then he gave her a kiss on the cheek. Both were enjoying the warm feeling of the early morning sunshine. They had fallen asleep on the swing and slept there all night. Neither could remember such a feeling of peace and serenity. They sat there enjoying the sounds of Mother Nature in the morning. Jeff looked over at Ruth, without her saying a word he said, "Yes darling, I agree. If nothing bad happens while we're here, let's move here for good". Ruth gave a smile to acknowledge Jeff's remark. They went inside and found both Angel and Nathan still asleep in bed. They took a shower and walked outside to enjoy Mother Nature again. The smell of steaks and ribs still lingered around the cabin.

Jeff said, "Let's take the scraps and do away with them before we have some unwanted guests."

Ruth replied, "What unwanted guests. You said we were five miles from the nearest house."

Jeff replied, "Yes honey, we are, but I'm talking about, wolves, coyotes and bears".

She replied, "Don't be silly. There are no bears within a hundred miles". They grabbed the scraps and walked towards the truck. Halfway between the truck and the stairs they heard a large growl. They turned to see what the noise was. A cold chill came over both of them. They reached over, took each other's hand and squeezed.

Jeff said, "You run, and I will deal with this".

She replied, "Not a chance, you go, I go". A few feet away were two of the biggest brown bears that they had ever seen. Each one must have been 7 foot tall and weighed 600 pounds or better. As the bears slowly approached they growled and bared their teeth at Jeff and Ruth. Ruth began to say the Lord's Prayer. At that instance the two bears let out a scream. Not a roar, but a scream. They went into a full charge. They ran straight at Jeff and Ruth. Jeff did the only thing he knew to do to protect Ruth. He stepped in front of her pushing her to the ground in the process. Both bears hit Jeff at a full run. Jeff went soaring backwards a good eight feet.

When Jeff opened his eyes, he could hear the two bears still screaming as they tore through woods. Jeff reached over to help Ruth up. They could still see the two bears running down the trail in a full run. It appeared they were looking back. Jeff and Ruth turned toward the stairs, and realized Angel and Nathan had come outside. They wondered how long they had been standing there. Angel was standing beside Nathan. Both were waving their hands at the bears. All of a sudden they heard a large crash, then the roar of one of the bears. Once on the deck, they started checking each other for wounds and injuries. Jeff realized he had probably received two broken ribs from the impact. Ruth was shaken up and dirty from the fall but had no injuries. A minor detail from the incident, Jeff realized that he was not only covered with dirt, there was bear droppings all over him. Apparently the bears had the same reaction to Nathan that all the other animals in his past had. The sight of Nathan literally scared the crap out of the bears.

The next day, Jeff decided to walk down the trail to the boat house. About one hundred yards down the trail, he spotted a huge bear. He stopped, trying not to make a sound. After a few seconds, he saw a small raccoon run in front of the bear. The bear did not move. Jeff took a few steps. Still, the bear did not move. He proceeded to approach the bear. It was suddenly obvious. The bear was dead. It was one of the two bears from yesterday. There was a visible chunk of bark missing from the tree. It appeared the bear had run into a large oak tree and broke his neck. By the condition of the tree, and the placement of the dead bear, Jeff figured the bears were too busy looking back and not watching where they were going. Thus, this one had hit the tree head on and the tree won. He walked back to their log home and told Ruth what he had seen. They decided not to venture towards that area again.

For the next four days Jeff, Ruth, Angel and Nathan enjoyed the peace and serenity. Ruth went outside and took several pictures of the log home and the surrounding area. Reality hit. It was time to go back home, back to their reality. They sat down on the couch in the log home and told Angel and Nathan that it was time for a family talk. Jeff and Ruth explained to the children that no one but them knew about this place. We have had our share of negative and unusual dilemmas; so understand this, never tell anyone about this place. In the years to come, if anything ever happens to me or your mother and you need a place to escape or hide, this is it. There are enough non-perishable foods to sustain you for a long time. Also, there is a hidden safe in the bathroom. The combination to the safe is your birth date. Also in the safe is a large sum of money that will last you a long time as well. In addition to that there is a letter and our account number to the bank. If anything were to happen to both of us, or we are killed in a car wreck, the lawyer handling our estate has been instructed, as well as the insurance company to direct deposit all of the money from the policies. That will be enough to last both of you a lifetime. As a reminder your mom has taken a picture of this place. She is going to put it above the mantel. Under the picture there will be a wooden plaque. The plaque will read "Remember". They packed up and headed home not knowing what wonderful turmoil and chaos awaited them.

Upon their arrival back home, they found a strange item in their yard. Jeff looked over at Ruth and said, "On any other given day this might seem bad".

Ruth smiled and said, "Honey, I would have been worried and disappointed if there wasn't something in the yard". Both of them looked at each other and began laughing. They unloaded the truck and trailer and sat down on the couch. Ruth said, "Honey, aren't you forgetting something?" He got up, went to the front yard, starred, and started laughing again. After a few more seconds, he reached over and pulled up the wooden cross that was placed upside down in the front yard and threw it in the back of his truck. He went back inside to enjoy the rest of the night. Both Angel and Nathan went straight to bed.

The next day Ruth placed the picture of their log home on the mantel, and Jeff placed the wooden plaque below it reading, "Remember". Once again Jeff and Ruth reminded Angel, if anything happens to us you know where to take Nathan. No one will ever find you there. Jeff started going through their stack of mail. One letter stood out, it was from the judge. Not wanting to ruin the plans he had made for Ruth's surprise birthday dinner, Jeff laid the letter to the side, knowing the contents would not be good news. Jeff had made plans to take Ruth out for her birthday to a very ritzy restaurant. Time alone out with each other was something they very seldom got to do, about as rare as a solar eclipse. Jeff said, "Honey, I don't care, good or bad at home, we are going out for your birthday". The dinner reservations were made in another city so no one in the area would recognize them as the parents with the Satan child. For awhile they didn't think they would be able to go because they could not find a babysitter. While at work, they could spend a couple of hours away from the kids. Surely two hours for dinner would be possible.

Ruth got off work a little later than she had planned, so she was rushed trying to get ready. She had stopped and picked up a couple of movies. Maybe this would keep Angel and Nathan busy until they got back. Just in case, she left her cell phone number on the television. It had been so long since Jeff and Ruth had been out that getting ready was almost as exciting and the actual plans for the night. Ruth pulled out all the stops, taking extra care with every detail. Angel said, "Mom, Dad won't recognize you. Jeff called Ruth and told her he was almost home. When he pulled in the driveway, Ruth was waiting for him on the porch. When Jeff saw Ruth all dressed up, he forgot to hit the brakes and ran into the garage. Man, she was hot. Jeff was so mesmerized he could hardly drive to the restaurant. They arrived at the restaurant safely, and Jeff let them valet park the car. He took Ruth's arm and proudly escorted her into the restaurant. As she walked through the restaurant, she turned several heads. Two waiters poured drinks into the laps of two patrons. Neither noticed the spill due to the fact they were watching Ruth also. She had the attention of every man in the place each and every one of them having thoughts of soft hugs and kisses. They were taken to the table that had been reserved for them. When she sat down at the table, you could almost hear two different sighs. One coming from the men in a sound of disappointment, the other from the women, the sound of relief that she was already taken. Admit it, men don't exactly look at what type of clothing a woman is wearing, but rather how well the clothing fits them. Waiters were arguing over who would wait on the table where Ruth was seated.

The women in the restaurant continued looking. Several of them had very confused looks on their faces. Some had faces of despair. Others were curling their noses and making strange faces. One thing about it, Ruth was with no doubt the hottest woman there. She was currently the center of attention. Their waiter was assigned and approached the table. While he was giving them the specials and taking their drink orders, he had a strange look come over his face. He could not take his eyes off Ruth. After taking their order he headed to the kitchen. Other waiters said, "You lucky dog. It's days like this that make coming to work worthwhile.

The waiter said, "Well, I thought I'd seen everything until now." He told the other waiters what he had seen. They began to snicker. They accused him of having one Bud Light to many. He told them, "If you don't believe me, go look for yourself". One by one, they made an excuse to go by Ruth's table to see if he had been telling the truth.

Once all the waiters had made the round, one asked, "Do you think she's in a cult?"

The others replied, "I don't know".

One lady in the restaurant called the waiter over and said, "I want to speak to the manager, and I mean right now".

The manager came out and asked, "Yes, may I help you".

The lady said, "Yes, we've been coming here for many years, and I want something done about that couple at the table".

The manager said, "Lady, I'm sorry your husband has not taken his eyes off of her, but neither has any other man. In fact several women have not taken their eyes off of them. Lady, let's face it, she is hot".

She grabbed the manager by the front collar, pulled him down, and whispered into his ear. she let him go.

He rose up and said, "Yes Ma'am". The manager slowly walked over to Jeff and whispered something in his ear. Jeff politely got up; reached down offering his hand to Ruth, he took her hand in his and helped her up from the table. With her hand in his, he escorted her to the exit, and they left.

When she got in the car she looked over at him and said, "Ok, what is going on?" He turned to her, took her hand in his and gently told her what the waiter said. Ruth began to cry. Then she threw up in the floor board of the car. After regaining her composure, they went home.

Back at the restaurant some women were still complaining to the manager about Ruth. Let's just say they were highly irritated. To calm them down the manager did the only thing he knew to do. He gave everyone their meals free, plus a free meal on their next visit. The women said, "Free, we can live with that".

Upon returning home Jeff helped Ruth inside. He sat her down on the couch and made her fresh coffee. Still crying, Ruth took her coffee, and headed to the bathroom to take a shower. She stopped in the hall and looked back at Jeff and said, "Well, you know what has to be done. If you love me take care of it right now." Jeff went to the car, picked up her fur coat from the back seat and threw it in the garbage.

After getting out of the shower she looked at Jeff and said, "I will never go out again, I'm so ashamed". You see, Ruth was in fact the hottest lady in the place, but like I said, men don't look at what a woman is wearing, but women do. In Ruth's rush to get ready; she didn't take a 100% inventory of her wardrobe. Her fur coat had an extra accessory on it. Not many women can gracefully wear a dead cat, skinned, with its tongue still hanging out of its mouth with a slight trace of blood still visible on the end of the tongue.

At some point Nathan had decided to exercise all nine lives of the cat at one time. After doing so, he apparently threw the cats hide over Ruth's fur coat to dry. In her haste to get ready, she never noticed the cat thrown on her fur coat.

Early the next morning, Jeff and Ruth were awakened by a knock at the door. Jeff answered the door. When he opened the door, there stood four police officers. One officer's handed Jeff a paper and said, "We have a court order to take Nathan back to the mental facility, now". Someone told the Judge That they had seen Nathan in the back yard, he immediately called the chief for action to be taken. The judge was not a happy camper. Jeff went upstairs to get Nathan and bring him back down stairs. The officer's hand cuffed Nathan. Before Jeff had a chance to say anything they were gone. Four police officers had arrived to transport Nathan back to the mental facility. Tell me they were not terrified of Nathan. Nathan was returned to the facility without incident.

Chapter eight

Six months had passed since Nathan had been returned to the facility. The community seemed to be settling back into a normal routine. That afternoon the judge was opening his mail and found a package from the hospital where Nathan was being kept. Along with the quarterly report that he had demanded, was a request for a weekend pass to go home with his family at their next visit. This infuriated him. Everything was just getting back to normal. He decided to take matters into his own hands. Rumors had surfaced at one time about some un-ethical friends he had been seen associating with. He spent the rest of the afternoon on the phone with a few of these friends. After several phone conversations and a few shady deals, he found a hospital that was willing to take Nathan. There were no surprises. The judge didn't hold anything back when describing the chaos that followed Nathan. He even went so far as getting a list of all the facilities that Nathan had been in and requested his medical files. These would be provided to the new doctors. It took a week for the medical records to arrive from the numerous facilities that Nathan had been placed in. He was horrified at some of the information inside these files, but she had made a decision and decided to stick with it. The community did not need anything like this living among them. The judge boxed all the files up and placed a cover letter in with the files that basically said use these as you see fit. The judge finally responded to the request for the pass for Nathan. He denied the request and informed the hospital and Nathan's parents that Nathan would be moved to another facility within 7 days. Arrangements were made between the facilities in regards to how the transfer would take place. Arrangements were made with the local Sheriffs' department to transfer Nathan to the new facility.

Even though the doctor had talked with the judge, when the bus pulled up and Nathan was escorted inside the side door where the doctor was waiting, he was still not prepared for what he saw. The doctor accepted all the transfer paperwork and took it to his office to read. He called Nathan's parents to let them know he had arrived safely and said they could visit Nathan in three months. This would allow them to get a proper evaluation of Nathan. After reading Nathan's file the doctor took Nathan to a solitary confinement hall and locked Nathan in his room until he could decide what to do. Shift change for the nurses was at two a.m. The hospital staff had not been informed about the transfer, therefore they had no idea what they were about to encounter. Breakfast was served at 6.00 a.m. The food was prepared and trays were loaded on the buggy for delivery to the patients' rooms. When the nurse arrived at room 13 which just happened to be Nathan's room she unlocked the door and went inside to deliver Nathan's food. When she turned and saw Nathan, she stopped suddenly. Silence was broken by an ear piercing scream. The sound of a food tray was heard crashing to the floor. Several nurses rushed to room 13 to see what was wrong. When the nurses entered Nathan's room they were shocked. A janitor almost ran into a nurse he was running so fast to see what had happened. When the janitor turned and saw Nathan he paused for about four seconds. Then he busted out laughing. It was like the domino effect. One after the other, the nurses started laughing. When Nathan stood up and seemed to stare at the nurses. The laughter suddenly stopped and the nurses backed out of the room. The janitor was told to clean up the mess.

Nathan was not brought a replacement tray. The word spread at the hospital. Nurses from all over the hospital made it a point to stop by and take a look at Nathan through the window portal of Nathan's door. The nurses on his hall decided one thing. They were not going to go anywhere around him or enter his room. This was defiantly not on their list of things to do. The nurses got together and bribed the janitor to deliver his food. The only problem was the janitor only worked from six a.m. to three p.m. The last meal of the day was at five p.m. This would mean that Nathan would only get food twice a day.

As far as the nurses on the other shifts, they also decided not to go in room 13. So once again, Nathan had been exiled from any contact with anyone. Day and night Nathan was left locked in his room. The only contact with anyone was with the janitor. Now to make things worse when the janitor would bring Nathan's food in, he would taunt and tease Nathan to no end. On top of that, he would eat whatever he wanted off of Nathan's plate and leave what he did not want. Nathan never had any dessert or pastry at all. The janitor always made sure to eat that. The only time Nathan got to eat his dessert was when his parents were visiting, and only if one of them stayed in the room while he did. Any time Nathan left dessert in his room during the family visit it was always gone when Nathan and Angel returned to the room. This went on for months and months.

During one family visit the doctor requested that Angel stay in the room with Nathan so he could talk to their parents. As the doctor was leaving Nathan's room Angel told him that the nurses and janitor were mean to Nathan. The doctor replied, "So what". The doctor informed Jeff and Ruth that they were doing everything they could, but so far there had been no noticeable change in Nathan's condition. But, just to be honest, they had no idea what to do or where to begin on treating their son. They told Jeff and Ruth that they had never seen anything like Nathan before. Nathan had been with them eight months and they had not been able to help him or had no clue where to start. They suggested their son would be much better off in another facility. While Jeff went to get Nathan and Angel, Ruth talked with the doctor about the condition of Nathan's room. When Jeff returned with Nathan and Angel they walked outside into the back area which was called the exercise yard. This was a fenced in area so the patients could enjoy the outdoors and sunlight.

The only time Nathan ever got to see this was once when the family visited. This was only his second time outside. In his eight months at this facility.

While Jeff and Ruth waited outside with Nathan, the doctor ordered the nurses and janitor to do a major clean-up and sanitize Nathan's room. He wanted to make sure the parents were satisfied so there would not be any surprise visits. This was only the second time that the nurses had been in Nathan's room since he had been incarcerated there. When they closed the door, they noticed paintings and drawings on the wall. These were not just ordinary drawings. They were specific and detailed. They noticed a sheet covering the inside of the door. When they removed it, there was a sense of amazement at first then an eerie feeling settled on them. The pictures drawn on the door were of the hospital staff, the doctor, and at the top of the door was a drawing of the janitor. These were more detailed than the others. These were more life-like than any photo ever taken of them that they had ever seen. Their names were written under each drawing.

One of the nurses asked, "How did he do these?" Once again, the drawings appeared to be in what they thought was human blood. The nurses stopped and looked at each other with confusion. The only thing that Nathan had in his room other than a bed was one red fire truck and a Television. When the nurses showed the doctor he was so astonished that he got his camera and took photos of everything in Nathan's room. He planned on placing them in Nathan's file and taking them home to show his wife.

The doctor found the family outside enjoying the sunshine and asked to talk to Jeff and Ruth again.

Angel and Nathan were taken back to his room while the doctor talked to her parents in his office. They went to get Angel and said their goodbyes to Nathan. They assured him they would be back when they could. On the way home the family had very little to say about Nathan. The next morning the doctor went back into Nathan's room to admire the drawings. This time there was something new on the inside of the door. Someone had written something. The doctor went back to get his camera and took more pictures to add to his file. This is what was written.

Behold these eyes
How lifeless how still
Destined for immortality
Destined to kill
You imprisoned his son
Isolated from all mankind
It's calm before the storm
Revenge is sweet as wine.
Enjoy your days
Relish your time
Satan is among us
He'll not be as kind
Gather your thoughts
Cherish them well
He's reserved a spot for you
To spend eternity in **HELL.**

After word of the writings spread throughout the facility the taunting became even worse. The nurses took this as a threat against their lives. How dare this little devil threaten them, just who in the hell did he think he was? When the nurses tried to get the other patients to make fun of Nathan they turned away and walked back to their rooms. Even though this facility was meant for the criminally insane, it seemed the patients had enough sense to stay away and leave Nathan alone. As you might expect there was no relief for little Nathan. The nurses and janitor would not hear of it. Once again, Nathan was moved to an isolated room with no TV, air conditioning, or heat. This is where Nathan would stay, until his parents would visit. At that time Nathan would once again be put in a regular room. The staff took extra precautions to make sure no one saw Nathan during these moves.

Once every two years the facility would host a family day. This was set up in hopes that it might improve the quality and attitude for the patients and to see how they would react with other people. Each patient was monitored and their actions recorded. Extra security was brought in just in case something was to happen. The back yard was full of people laughing and having a good time, or at least they were until Nathan and his family came through the door to the yard. When Nathan entered the yard, everyone stopped and just stared at him. This was the first time any of the family members had ever seen him. No one had ever seen a child like this. It was as if everyone had been put into a state of suspended animation.

Three of the nurses told the janitor to take Angel and the devil child back inside before he ruined the whole day. The janitor walked up and told Angel she would have to take snowflake back inside. He escorted them back to Nathan's room. He taunted them saying, "No one wants to see this little freak of nature". Angel did not say a word. A couple of hours had passed when screams broke the silence in the facility. The noise was coming from room 13. The echo from the hallway pierced the yard. Everyone including the visitors started running towards the commotion. There stood Angel crying. There stood the janitor, shouting and screaming at Nathan. There stood Nathan covered in blood.

When one of the nurses screamed, Nathan turned around. He held his arms out with his hands open and palms up with blood dripping off his fingers. Hanging from the bathroom curtain rod was two of the facilities beloved pet cats, or what was left of them. It appeared Nathan had taken the two pet cats and tied their tails together. The carnage was really bad. It's hard to believe that two little cats can produce so much blood. This time the scene was a little different. This time it appeared that Nathan had taken two muzzles and put over the cat's mouth so he could watch them claw each other longer instead of them biting each other.

This time within a few hours phone calls smothered the facility. This time it was lawyers representing family members of the patients that were incarcerated at the facility. When the Lawyer's said one word, "lawsuit". That was enough for the doctor.

The Doctor contacted the judge that was handling Nathan's case and strongly recommended that Nathan be transferred to another facility. He wanted this devil child moved. He didn't care where, just moved now and today. The judge agreed but said he would take a little while to process the paper work and make the necessary arrangements.

Early the next morning Nathan's family returned to the facility to check and see how Nathan was doing. While the doctor discussed Nathan's future or lack of with the parents, Angel stayed with Nathan in his room. Without anyone noticing, Angel had sneaked Nathan a piece of pastry in his room. For some unknown reason someone had left Nathan's door unlocked. Angel took Nathan's hand and went walking down the hall. Within a few minutes one of the nurses spotted them in the hall. This was unacceptable. The nurse paged the doctor and told him about Nathan being out of his room. The doctor cornered Nathan and Angel at the hall exit leading to the back yard. He told Angel that Nathan was not allowed out of his room. He escorted them back to room 13. Just as they were turning the corner of the hall, they saw the janitor leaving Nathan's room. When Angel and Nathan went in the room, Angel noticed half of Nathan's pastry was gone. Obviously the janitor had taken it. The doctor told Angel to wait in the lunch room for a few minutes while he talked to Nathan. About twenty minutes later one of the nurses took Angel back to Nathan's room. A few minutes later the janitor returned to Nathan's room as well. He looked at Nathan and said, "Hey freak, this pastry is way too good for the likes of you and swallowed it all in one bite". When he turned around, he saw Angel. He didn't think no one would be in the little freak's room. He just looked at her and said it's time for you to go.

By this time it was shift change. Nathan's family said their goodbyes and left for home. Hours had passed. One of the nurses walked by Nathan's room and she noticed a liquid easing out from under Nathan's door. She paged the doctor and could not get an answer. She went to the nurses desk, got another nurse and the key to Nathan's room. When she tried to open the door to Nathan's room, it would not move. She and the other nurse tried to open the door, but to no avail. They called two other nurses to help and try to open the door. They all gave a big push. The door opened. Whatever was blocking the door was not blocking it any more. Reluctantly they entered Nathan's room. Screams and cries filled the hallway once again. Numerous nurses and facility staff converged on room 13 to see what all the commotion was about.

There inside Nathan's room lying behind the door was the janitor. Coming from his mouth was the liquid that the nurses had seen coming from under Nathan's door. As well as what appeared to be some type of pastry. The janitor was dead. In a case like this protocol orders a complete shut down of the facility. Nobody was allowed in except key personnel and absolutely no one out.

Once again, police were called to the scene. The doctor immediately ordered test results on the pastry and also an autopsy of the janitor. Everything was at a stand still, until the results came back. When the test came back on both, they were compared. Both showed considerable traces of rat poison but not just any rat poison. It just so happened to be the same kind that was used in the facility. This was enough. Somehow this little demonic freak had acquired rat poison. "No more", the nurses shouted.

With a police escort, the nurses along with the police took Nathan back to the very last room in the basement where no one ever goes. There they locked Nathan in a room with no lights, TV, water, bed, or even a bathroom. The only thing in the room was an old drain basin that was located in the middle of the room, nothing else. The nurses went back to room 13. There they were going to try and clean up the mess. When they closed the door they all stood there and gasped. Tears rolled down their faces. Remember the pictures that were painted on the inside of the door of the staff and janitor. Well, now something new had been added. The picture of the janitor had a red X placed over his face. Right then and there, the nurses decided as far as they were concerned that Nathan could stay down there and starve to death. They decided not one of them would go down in the basement and feed that freak of nature.

On the third evening a fax was received. It was the order of the judge sending Nathan to another facility. The one thing that scared the nurses the most was what would Nathan do to them if he did escape from the basement. They called the police. Three officers and three nurses were sent down into the basement. Slowly they opened the freezing, cold, dark room where Nathan had been forgotten about for three wonderful days. There he sat with his back to the door on the cold wet floor. You would think that three police officers and three nurses would not be terrified of a little boy. Well, these six adults were.

The new facility and the doctors were waiting on little Nathan. In the final report they had received from the mental doctor the following was highlighted. It is my professional opinion that Nathan should never be allowed back into society. If he is released, mark my words. Death and destruction will follow for anyone who crosses his path. The **devil** is in him.

One of the houses that Jeff and his family had lived in years ago was on the market for sale. A young couple with two children had bought the house and moved in. This is their brief story. Three months after moving in, their two children were playing in the basement. Then their mom called and said time for dinner. The two children walked into the kitchen. Suddenly their mom shouted, "You go right now and wash those filthy hands."

After coming from the bathroom their dad said, "How did you get so dirty".

They replied, "They had been playing in the basement." He had a strange look on his face.

After dinner was over he told his wife, "I'm going to check the basement."

Hs wife asked. "Why".

He said "Honey, the basement is supposed to have a solid foundation". He walked down the stairs. After twenty or thirty minutes, Dad came walking back into the upstairs bathroom. He had a really strange look on his face. Some of his color was gone.

When his wife asked, "What's the matter",

He said, "It's not good, you don't need to go down there, I've already told the kids to stay out of the basement. Being curious, she walked down in the basement. Within a few minutes, once again silence was broken at the house, a really loud scream and crashing sound. Just a couple of minutes later, mom walked back in the upstairs bathroom, took a cold wash cloth, and began to wash her face.

She looked over at dad and said, "What are we going to do?"

Dad said, "We have to go to the police".

Mom said, "You know this is not going to be good".

Dad made the phone call. He said, "I need a officer here at this address ASAP".

The dispatcher asked, "is this an emergency," and He said, "no, not now". The dispatcher confused with Jeff's answer called an officer to respond to the residence.

When the officer asked the dispatcher if it was an emergency she replied, "Not now".

The confused officer stepped on the pedal, especially after receiving the location. This officer had responded to this address on numerous occasions before when Jeff and Ruth lived there. Upon arriving at the address, the officer approached the house using extreme caution. At that moment he stepped on the front step, when he did the door popped open. The officer reached for his weapon. He unsnapped his gun ready for the worse. Dad opened the door and introduced himself.

The officer said, "How can I help and how bad is it?"

Dad said, "Sounds like you've been here before". The officer asked, "How could he help."

Dad said, "Well, when was the last time he ate".

The officer replied, "I haven't eaten today".

Dad said, "Well you might be ok, you need to take a look in the basement". The officer went cautiously down in the basement. Having the unlucky pleasure of having to respond to this house many times before, he was expecting the worse. After hitting the bottom of the basement, he was still not ready for what he was about to see.

A large voice came echoing from the basement, "holy crap.". The officer came back looking pale and sickly. He said with a struggle in his voice, "Do not go back down there, stay the hell out. He went to his car and made a call. He took a chair and sat down, blocking the entrance to the basement. Once again silence was broken. Three police cars filled the driveway along with a crime scene van. Men dressed in white jumpers and carrying shovels and cameras and officers carrying plastic bags entered the house wearing white masks.

One officer wearing captains insignias asked the officer blocking the basement door, "are you sure?"

And he replied, "Have at it, I'll wait here." Six people entered the basement. A variety of words came from the basement that we won't repeat. Three hours passed with clanging and beating. Then footsteps, three men came running from the basement. Following them was an indescribable stench, an odor which would bring tears to your eyes.

Dad said, "Well what's the damage"?

One officer replied, "34 cats and 2 dogs so far, buried in the north side of the basement."

Dad said, "Man you sure have brought a lot of people."

The officer replied, "Plus the remains of two humans buried under the two dogs".

Dad asked, "Who are they".

The officer replied, "We don't know, and we may never know due to the decomposition of the bodies."

Once again neighbors filled the street just like so many times before. The sight was chaos. Bags and bags of bones were being removed from the basement. Neighbors stood and watched. One neighbor replied,

"Well, at any other house that might be shocking, but here it's normal".

Dad asked, "How soon can we get back to normal in our house"?

The officer started laughing and said, "Now, we're done here. Unless you find more bodies or bones buried or hidden on the property".

The officer also replied, "Sir, there is nothing normal about this address. Good luck". Dad didn't think that was funny, but the office was serious.

They did in fact find out the names of 18 of the cats according to their collars. The two dogs were later identified in the same manner. It was rumored the two bodies were the owners of the two dogs; their owners had been missing with the two dogs in the same time frame. The findings though were never conclusive. The two men that were actually missing at some point in time, worked for the pest control company that had a contract to spray for bugs back when Jeff and Ruth lived there. Autopsy later revealed both men and two dogs were poisoned and beaten to death. The perpetrator would never be found or recognized. Dad did not look for anymore bones. He simply propped the basement window open. Poured the floor and sides with concrete, This was to help prevent any more surprises. It worked. This would be the last record ever processed on this previous residence.

Rumors at the local barber shop and beauty salon were out of control. Rumors and other events seemed to be growing faster than cud zoo vines in the south.

Buy now Jeff and his family had acquired the ultimate reputation of animal cruelty, torture, and even the leaders of a sadistic cult. Some neighbors told of stories of mayhem and violence, and blood curlding events so horrific that the devil himself would have cold chills and might even get a bit squeamish.

Things were starting to relax once again. Jeff had called the facility where little Nathan was incarcerated to give them their new phone number.

Two months have passed since their relocation. Early that morning Jeff and Ruth received a phone call from the mental facility where Nathan was incarcerated. Upon answering the phone, Jeff and Ruth were told that Nathan was being given a one week pass to come home. No matter how hard this family tried, it seemed that life would never give them peace of mind. Jeff, Ruth and Angel went to pick up Nathan at the facility. Before they left, they decided it best not to come home but try one more week at their cabin. With all things considered except for the bear incident, it was a pretty good vacation. So, to the cabin they headed. It took several hours for the drive. By the time they reached the cabin it was getting close to dark. Upon arrival, they unloaded the van. By this time it was dark. Jeff and Ruth kept hearing the cracking of leaves in the woods around the cabin. Each time Jeff shined the flashlight through the bedroom window, he was never able to see anything. Jeff stayed up most of the night concerned about the sounds coming from outside the cabin. At some point, during the early morning hours, Jeff did fall asleep. When Ruth woke up she knew Jeff had a long night. So she decided to be real quiet and let him sleep. You could not have asked for a better morning. The sun had broken the horizon. The rays of sun glistened off the lake below. Peace and quiet was at its best ever.

This time a blood curling scream came from Ruth. Jeff came running to the kitchen from where the screams echoed through the cabin. When Jeff reached the kitchen he shouted, "What's wrong?"

Ruth replied, "We are in big trouble, look out the window".

When Jeff saw what Ruth was screaming about, he said, "Honey, don't worry, we'll figure something out."

She replied, "How, we are done for, we're going to die here."

Jeff replied, "It could be worse."

Ruth shouted, "Honey it doesn't get worse than this." About that time Angel came down the stairs and asked, "What was wrong."

Ruth said, "Look outside."

"Oh my word," Angel replied. Turned and ran back upstairs to get Nathan. Within a couple of minutes she brought Nathan downstairs and headed towards the front door.

Jeff shouted, "No, do not open that door", Angel did anyway and took Nathan on the front porch of the cabin. When they got to the steps she told Nathan to raise his hands. When he did, the ground shook and a path was cleared. Surrounding the cabin there must have been ten thousand snakes of all kinds and sizes. It seems that from the beginning of time, snakes have symbolized the negative of life. Snakes symbolized evil. Well, at least the snakes were at the right place. It looked like every snake within a twenty mile radius had come to pay their respects to little Nathan. When Nathan raised his hands, the snakes not only cleared a path for them to walk, but it appeared they were bowing their heads as well. Needless to say Jeff and

Ruth seized the moment of a clear path. Bewildered, they followed Nathan to the van watching as the snakes cleared a path as they walked. When they reached the van and looked back they realized the snakes had closed the path behind them. They cleared the mountain of snakes. It was obvious they would never return here again, or at least not with Nathan. No one would believe the snakes so Ruth took a picture. Even seeing the picture, it's hard to fathom and understand, how and why all the snakes just happen to show up at the cabin.

For the next four days, they rented a room in a motel at the base of the mountain. Only Jeff would leave to go get the necessary supplies, and food. They knew they couldn't return home with Nathan. After Nathan's one week pass was up they returned him to the facility where he would remain until further notice. Before they left the facility, Nathan's doctor told them not to call for four months.

Three houses above Jeff lived Mr. Jones and his family. The Jones family had been out of town for a few days visiting family. Upon returning home, Mr. Jones noticed his front door to the house was not as he had left it. Mr. Jones told his wife to keep the children in the car until he had checked and cleared the house to make sure that there were no unwanted guests in the house. He checked every room and could not find anything, but he forgot to check the attic and basement. Usually that's where the bad stuff happens. After clearing the house Mr. Jones allowed his wife April and their two children into the house. They emptied their luggage, put away their belongings, and sat down to enjoy a relaxing evening at home.

At some point that night they went to bed. The next morning breakfast was a big hit. They reflected back on their peaceful vacation. After breakfast the children watched TV while April and Shaun finished the breakfast dishes. Shaun said he was going to go and check the mail. April said she would put the luggage back in the basement until they needed it again.

As Shaun opened the mail box a blood curdling scream came from inside the house. At that point Shaun made a scramble to the front door. As he reached the door, he was distracted by another scream. At that moment he missed the step and tripped. In full motion Shaun hit the door head first. His momentum was such that he lay on the porch, just a frog hair from being completely knocked out. The two children ran to their Mom to see what was wrong. The children's screams reached Shaun who was still severely dazed from head butting the door as he staggered through the house as fast as he could towards the basement. Upon entering the basement, still trying to focus his vision another scream came from his wife, "April, "Help I'm in the basement you idiot."

Shaun staggered to the basement door. When he entered the basement, it was a sight of unimaginable carnage. When April turned to look at Shaun, she let out another scream. Shaun was covered in blood. Shaun never realized his injuries from the impact of his head hitting the door. She grabbed a towel to cover his face. So with her and the two children screaming and holding the towel on Shaun's face, they evacuated the basement. She escorted him back to the front of the house. By this time neighbors had already heard the screams and called 911. Well, par for the course, 911 had already received so many calls from that street that it was now standard procedure, when a call came in from "Killing Lane". They were to send everybody, police, fire dept, and medics, with the coroner on standby.

As April emerged through the front door, she was met by all the above. As medics rushed to give aid to Shaun, officers gathered information from April. The two officers on duty Randall and Tim knew not to go in any house on this street without an idea of what might be inside or without back-up. As medics triaged Shaun's injuries, one medic notated the injuries as another gave aid. Shaun had sustained a broken nose in three places. One small part of the bone was sticking from his nose. The big injury was a 6" gash to his cephalic region, or forehead, with small splinters protruding from his wound that he had collected from the front door.

Randall entered the basement first with Tim following. They were still unsure what April was trying to tell them. The closer they got to the basement steps, the slower they got. With guns drawn and flashlights in hand, they reached the bottom step. They couldn't fathom what they were seeing. Tim turned and ran back upstairs knocking two firemen off the porch as he made his exit. There the he fell to his hands and threw up on the front lawn. You could tell what he had eaten for the last three days.

Randall took photos of the carnage. Blood saturated all four corners of the basement. The chief entered the basement and shouted, "Cut that ceiling fan off." The noise stopped. Whether or not little

Nathan was responsible for this carnage didn't matter, he was getting the blame. The bottom line was the ceiling fan had six blades. Hanging from each blade was what was left of the children's six pets. It appeared little Nathan had tied their pets to the blades, took a knife and gutted them and turned the ceiling fan on high, slinging the blood, entrails, and other stuff against the floor and walls. Easter would never be the same again. Remember a rabbit's foot is supposed to be good luck. The ceiling fan had 24 rabbit's feet hanging from it, so much for good luck.

As neighbors stood outside the house trying to see what was going on, one of the neighbor's children started screaming and crying. "Now what?" one officer shouted. They were a total of eight rabbits that were supposed to be the children's pets. The neighbor's child had found the other two or what was left of them. It seemed that Nathan had buried the other two rabbits in the ground with the exception of their heads sticking up above ground level. Took one of the old manual push mowers with rotating blades and decapitated them. Police officers and neighbors converged on Jeff's house like bees after honey only to find no one at home. With no evidence to convict Nathan, he was never charged with the rabbit demolition scene.

Remember at the start of the book, how sometimes events or people have a way of interacting with each other in some form or manner throughout time. Back when Mr. Shaun Jones was a teenager, he had two childhood friends, Randall and Tim. One afternoon all three boys decided to sneak in Mrs. Milner's pond. To give you an idea of how she felt about her pond, when Mrs. Milner got remarried, it was in a written agreement that her new husband, Matt or any of his famil, would not be allowed to fish in her pond. Well, all three boys snuck in right at dusky dark. Shaun already had his rod and reel rigged up with a top water lure. Shaun made his first cast. He threw over next to some bull rush weeds on the deep end. About three cranks of the reel, a humongous largemouth bass attacked the top water lure and the fight was on. Randall and Tim ran over to help Shaun with this monster bass. Within a few seconds the bass busted the top of the water again. There was a small pine tree thicket that separated Mrs. Milner's house and the pond. All the sudden the sound of a screen door slammed against the house. A squeaky high pitched voice said, "Hey, whose fishing in my pond? I'm going to get my gun and shoot your butt". The screen door slammed again. A third screen door slammed and a loud boom. Shot gun pellets about tree top level. Randall and Tim commenced gathering their fishing gear. Meanwhile, Shaun was still fighting with the bass. Another loud boom, this time shot gun pellets came from about half way up the tree then the third boom. Randall looked over at Tim and said, "I'm right behind you," this time when the third boom went off; shot gun pellets were spraying the water. Randall and Tim took off. They stopped at the top of the hill, turned around, and watched Shaun still standing there fighting the large bass. They saw Mrs. Milner making her way towards the pond and Shaun. When she aimed the gun at them, they were gone.

When they reached the dirt road where they had left their truck, they turned around just in time to hear two more blast from the shot gun, and a loud scream. A couple of minutes had passed. Randall looked over at Tim, still no sign of Shaun. Tim said," We need to call the Police. I think she has killed Shaun". Then they saw a silhouette of a person running over the terrace rows in the pasture. Thank God, it was Shaun running with all he had. As he got closer, Randall and Tim could see he was slumped over. When he finally reached the truck, they were astonished at what they saw. First, Shaun had been running like a football player carrying a ball, but he was carrying the large mouth bass instead. The biggest bass they had ever seen. They weighed the bass at 14 lbs 3 oz. The second thing, Shaun was so excited about the big catch that he had not realized two things. One he forgot his rod and reel and left them back at the pond. Second, he did not realize how bad he was hurt and how much he was covered in blood. Randall shouted, "Oh my god, you've been shot".

They rushed Shaun home first so he could put the large bass in the gold fish tank. They called his Dad and took him to the hospital. After cleaning him up, they learned that during the process of Shaun running with the bass under his arm, the dorsal fin caught him good, in fact 15 stitches worth. After Shaun told his Dad what had happen, his Dad just smiled and said, "Well son, a lesson well learned" Shaun replied, "For darn sure, next time I'll make sure she's not at home".

Shaun's Dad replied, "Yep, yep, that's my boy".

Remember how we talked about reoccurring situations, the two officers who responded to Shaun's house during the rabbit incident, well, that was Randall and Tim, so it may be a small world after all.

Chapter nine

THE DISTRICT JUDGE RECEIVED so many phone calls about little Nathan that he thought it would be a good idea to move this little devil to another facility. The judge was tired of getting negative phone calls from family of the patients incarcerated where little Nathan was. Plus the staff at the facility was not cutting him any slack. Oh yes, let's don't forget election was right around the corner. That may have had a play in his decision as well. The judges game plan was to transfer little Nathan to another facility way out of his jurisdiction. And, so the order was given. After an extensive search Nathan's doctor found another facility about two hundred miles away. He had previously worked with the Director, Mr. Horton. The doctor called the judge and told him that they had found another facility stupid enough to take little Nathan. No time was wasted.

Early Monday morning two orderlies took Nathan to the van. They had him shackled, handcuffed, and a muzzle over his face. They were not taking any chances. While the van was en-route to the new facility, one of the nurses made a phone call. Her call was to the new facility where her sister Evelyn was on staff. She began to unload on her sister about the events and situations involving the "child of Satan". Her sister started laughing and thought it was a joke. No child could be as bad as this. Evelyn decided not to take any chances. Even the worst criminals were not as bad as her sister made little Nathan out to be. But, just in case, after their phone call was over, Evelyn began to inform the other staff members of what she had been told by her sister.

The van arrived at the facility at four pm. The Director, Mr. Horton and the Head nurse, Evelyn along with numerous staff were standing at the windows to catch a glimpse of this "devil child". When the van door opened, the security removed little Nathan from the van with all the hardware. Well, let's say you never have a second chance to make a first impression. Security escorted Nathan to the holding room and cuffed him to the bench. The transferee papers were signed. Like a flash of lightening, the doctor and security guard ran to the van. The nurses peeked around the corner at Nathan. Someone shouted. "What was this thing that was left at their door." Good news travels fast. But bad news travels faster. It wasn't long before the entire facility had received news of the freak, this child of Satan.

The first day little Nathan was put in a regular room. By the next morning all the staff and even some of the patients had visited Nathan's room. Three of the most dangerous criminals who were incarcerated at this facility made arrangements to visit this little freaks room. Mark, Axle, and Jonas did not take long to decide they wanted no part of this thing. There's an old saying that evil will recognize evil. Mark, Axle and Jonas knew right then they were out of their element. In a sense the three criminals ran the facility. What they had on the director no one ever knew. But Nathan was not something they wanted to deal with. They informed the staff and doctors if Nathan was not kept separate from the rest of the population there would be severe problems for everyone.

The head nurse did notice one thing about Nathan that no one had ever noticed before. Nathan had no finger nails or toe nails. Also, with the exception of his head there was not one hair on Nathan what so ever, when she told the other nurses of this, they were amazed. This excited Evelyn the head nurse to no end, so much that she began to visit little Nathan on a regular basis. Whatever she did to little Nathan we'll ever know. She assigned two orderlies, Jim and Ray, to watch Nathan.

They looked forward to the assignment and were already planning how they could make Nathan's stay miserable. One afternoon the orderlies were called to the front office. Both were concerned that they were in trouble for the way they had been treating Nathan. About ten minutes later they emerged from the office with a strange look on their face. They went to their locker and got a brown paper sack and their cooler. They had sneaked cattle prods into the facility in the brown paper bags. They immediately went to Nathan's dungeon. They sat down in lawn chairs one on each side of Nathan. They reached in their cooler and pulled out an ice cold Bud Light beer. With a Bud Light in one hand and a fully charged cattle prod in the other, they raised the bud light and tapped them for a toast on their raises for doing such a good job. They looked down at little Nathan and said this Bud's for you.

At the same time, while taking a drink of Bud, they hit Nathan with the cattle prods. One cattle prod hit Nathan on the left thigh. The other prod hit Nathan on the right thigh. They continuously held the prods on Nathan until they finished their Buds. Due to Nathan's white pearly skin, you could see the electrical charge run from one prod to another. After finishing their Buds, they reached down in the cooler and toasted another Bud, with electrical charge included once again. They repeated this until the beers were gone and so was the charge of the prods. With the cattle prods empty and the orderly's fully charged with beer. They left Nathan's dungeon to go upstairs, one orderly turned around and grabbed Nathan's water bowl. He left the room and brought the bowl back in full.

He looked at little Nathan and said, "Hey little buddy, don't you worry about the dingy look of your water. The pipes are leaking and it will soon clear back up". As he was leaving, he turned and said to Nathan, "We'll be back later this afternoon and play some more". As the orderlies reached the elevator, Jim turned to the other and said, "Hey Ray don't forget to zip up your pants". The dingy look was from Ray using the water bowl for a urinal.

Ray smiled and said, "Yep, payback is hell isn't it". The other orderly just smiled and said. "Yes sir it is". He never knew what Ray meant by the remark.

During little Nathan's incarceration in his dungeon, he went through torture, abuse, and other situations that we can't even imagine in our wildest dreams or nightmares. Yet, through the electric shock, filth, food that rats would not even eat, and high pressure water hose little Nathan survived.

He endured it all. He never made a sound, flinched, or tried to fight back. His torment was seven days a week. No one knew how many hours a day this went on. The orderlies enjoyed coming in to work just so they could have their fun with poor little Nathan. The orderlies were constantly trying to think of new ways to entertain themselves in torturing little Nathan. According to the nurses, numerous times they would come up from the dungeon with blood stains on their shoes and clothing. The Nurses gave the impression they did not care what happened down there as long as they did not have to fool with that little devil. The orderlies two favorite things they liked to do to little Nathan was as follows. First and foremost, there was a small doggie bowl that was bolted to the floor of the dungeon. The only way Nathan could get a drink of water was to get down on all fours like a little dog and lap up the water with his tongue like a little dog. When Nathan stuck his tongue in the bowl of water, the orderlies would stick the cattle prods in the water and discharge the electrical current. They always got a good chuckle from this because you could see the electrical current run from the water to his tongue. This would cause Nathan to have severe muscle spasms, and he would flop around on the floor like a fish out of water. Their second favorite thing to do was to strap Nathan's wrist and ankles to the eye bolts that were drilled in the floor of his dungeon. Take the high pressure water hose and vigorously hit him full blast. They would take the cattle prods and discharge them on the bottom of his feet and watch his toes curl up backwards. Sometimes to break up the routine they would take the cattle prods and place one of them at his left inside thigh and the other on the right inside thigh. At the same time they would discharge both cattle prods. They would hold the prods down until the batteries were dead. They would laugh because they said you could see the electrical charge run from one thigh to the other and meet in the middle. Well, you know where the middle is. This may be another reason little Nathan had no hair on his body. Remember, Nathan was not allowed to wear clothes in his dungeon. Therefore, the orderlies had easy access to any part of his body and a full view of his pearly white skin. This pearly white skin made it easier to see the electrical current as it would pass from one part of his body to the other. Since little Nathan never made a sound nor did he flinch or try to fight back, this may have increased the abuse and torture. Or, simply the orderlies just enjoyed it way too much.

There were rumors that a couple of nurses got in on the fun but only if the orderlies were present. The nurses enjoyed watching a certain part of Nathan's body wiggle when the cattle prods were discharged on each side of his groin area. They would run back up stairs and share their moments with the other nurses. It only took two days at the most for all the burn marks and puncture wounds to heal. Other than that two day time frame it was open season on little Nathan.

Ray C. hated the idea, but he was told to take vacation or lose it. So he took two weeks. While he was gone, it left Jim to take care of little Nathan. A visit from Nathan's family was long overdue. Jeff, Ruth and Angel arrived early that morning before the staff had time to make their rounds. When one of the nurses recognized Nathan's family, she paged the doctor. Well, the rush was on. The staff must have set a record trying to prepare a regular room for little Nathan. The Director was impressed. They fixed up a fantastic room with toys and a color TV. They rushed Nathan to his room. When Jeff and his family walked in it was WOW, all of this just for little Nathan. You would not believe the dinner that had been prepared for little Nathan. It included Rib eye steak, mashed potatoes, green beans, ice cold coke, fresh market rolls, and the best tasting chocolate cake you have ever seen, just for being such a good little boy. The mere sight of this made Ruth break out in tears. After their time was up for their visit Jeff and his family left. Within a few seconds of the family leaving the Jim drug Nathan back down to his dungeon. He went back upstairs and consumed the fantastic meal in Nathan's fake room. One of the nurses went to check to see what was taking him so long to finish the dinner. When she walked in the room, she screamed. There lay the orderly on the floor, DEAD. Chocolate cake hanging from his mouth. It was determined that the cake was laced with an excessive amount of rat poison. How in the world did Nathan get rat poison? Unless it had been left somewhere in Nathan's dungeon. The nurse did notice one more thing. Something had been written on the inside of the door. This is what was written:

> Behold these eyes
> How lifeless how still
> Destined for immortality
> Destined to kill
> Look closely ye mortals
> At his eyes of death
> This will be the last thing you see
> Upon your last breath
> You had your fun
> You had your time
> Enjoy your sad life
> Your soul will be mine
> Enjoy your days
> Few as they may be
> Soon when you open your eyes
> It's me you will see
> I won't forget
> The things you've done
> To poor little Nathan
> I'm **Satan**
> He is my **son**

The one thing that all the nurses had in common with each other was that they hated the head nurse Evelyn. The main reason was, she would come in late, leave early, and on several occasions could be found in Mr. Horton's office asleep. It was no secret that Evelyn and Mr. Horton were working overtime, but usually on each other. They were tired of being treated the way they were and her hateful attitude she had towards them. They had no one to complain to. Since Mr. Horton was the Director their hands were tied. But, now with the death of Jim, this could open a whole new can of worms. That is exactly what happened. One Monday morning just like many times before, Evelyn came in late and went straight to Mr. Horton's office, kicked back in his chair and went to sleep. Around 10:00 a.m. a stranger walked in looking around as if he was lost.

The charge nurse, Julie, approached the gentlemen and asked, "May I help you sir?"

The gentlemen said, "Yes, could you tell me where Mr. Horton's office is."

Julie replied, "Yes sir, its two doors down on the left at the end of the hall. May I take you there."

The gentlemen replied, "Yes, if you would please."

Julie asked, "Are you friends with Mr. Horton?"

The gentlemen replied, "No ma'am, my name is Shaun and I have never met the man before in my life." And he left it at that. Julie escorted the gentlemen to Mr. Horton's office. When they reached the office, he reached inside his pocket, pulled out a key and unlocked the door. Upon opening the door he sees a female laying back in the chair with her feet propped on the desk and in deep sleep. With arms crossed, Shaun watches her for a few minutes, He turns to Julie ask, "Who is that and what is she doing in MY OFFICE.?

Julie replied, "Sir, that is Mrs. Evelyn, the head nurse, and I don't understand when you say your office."

Shaun told her, "Mr. Horton will no longer be working here. He has been reassigned to another location."

Julie asked, "Why?"

Shaun replied, "The state board received numerous phone calls and letters about some of the questionable activity that was taking place here. So after an extensive investigation, the board decided that Mr. Horton did not need this job after all. I am the new Director."

Julie asked, "Sir, if you don't mind me asking are you planning on making any changes?"

Shaun looked over at Julie and smiled and looked back over at Evelyn and said, "Well, Julie I'm looking at one right now setting in my chair." He closed the door rather hard.

Mrs. Evelyn jumped up and asked, "What the hell are you doing in my office?" She began to chew Julie out for letting this person in her office without permission. Julie just stood there trying not to laugh as Evelyn kept on sticking her foot in her mouth.

Shaun said, "I thought this was the director's office." Mrs. Evelyn began to tell him off, and let him know that she was in charge here. She made the rules.

Shaun said, "Lady I don't need your permission to be in this office." Evelyn came unraveled. She screamed at Shaun, picked up the phone and called security. It went out over the loud speaker for security come to the Directors office immediately. Not only did security come to the Director's office but a few other staff came running as well. When all were in the room, Evelyn bowed up and said, "Get this idiot out of here, and right now."

The chief of security said, "We can't." Before he could explain, Evelyn screamed, "You're all fired."

Julie spoke up and said, "Everyone, I would like you to meet our new Director Mr. Shaun."

When Julie said that, you could see a smile on everyone's face except for Evelyns'. You could literally see the color draining right out of her body. Shaun asked for a few minutes alone with Evelyn. She tried her best to act like she had been joking. When that did not work she tried picking up with Shaun where she had been with Mr. Horton by offering sexual favors. Shaun let her know right then that he was not or ever would be interested. Changes were made. Julie is now enjoying her new position as head nurse. Evelyn was demoted. Evelyn was so mad that she decided to turn her aggression towards Nathan. She began strapping Nathan to the bed and would take a wooden spoon and other objects and spank the bottom of his feet, stopping just at the point of them bleeding. This went on for some time, until, Shaun and Julie walked in on her abusing Nathan. Security was called and Evelyn was escorted out of the building. Julie had the wonderful task of mailing her the pink slip along with her last paycheck.

After settling in to his new position as Director he pulled numerous case files and found numerous cases of severe abuse and neglect from several of the doctors on staff. You've heard the term, cleaning house. This is exactly what he did. He fired several doctors and brought in a new staff. He had worked with these doctors and knew them personally. He knew these doctors would treat the staff and patients like they were supposed to. He was especially disturbed after reviewing Nathan's case file. He could not believe the other director or doctors had allowed this type of treatment.

Jeff, Ruth and Angel arrived home one Sunday, late in the afternoon after a weekend getaway. While they had been gone, a message had been left on their answering machine to give the hospital where Nathan was a call. When they returned the phone call, they were put in direct contact with the new Director, Shaun. Shaun informed them about the changes that had been made and the new doctors that were taking over Nathan's case. They were very happy. Just the way he spoke to them gave them hope. He asked them to be patient and as soon as they had time they would contact them on what they found out about Nathan from the new test that were about to be given. This might give the new doctors a chance to give them a new status on their son.

After numerous tests, the doctors finally had something positive to report. The doctors finally had some answers as to why Nathan was the way he was. An MRI of the brain, neck, and chest revealed damage to his larynx. The diagnosis was that he had Laryngeal nerve damage. Injury to the nerves is usually the cause, but since it appeared at birth the doctors presumed that the damage was caused by a viral infection in-vitro that affected the nerves. This is why he could not speak or ever cried. One of the specified treatments for this was injections of collagen. While the doctors were drawing blood and running test, they noticed that Nathan never flinched or seemed to notice any pain. They observed him for a few days in different situations. One of the doctors remembered an article he had read recently about a child who couldn't feel pain. The article was about congenital insensitivity to pain (CIP). CIP is a rare and often fatal condition that affects under 100 people in the United States each year. The doctors were amazed that Nathan had survived this long, because this disorder kills most while they are still toddlers. There is no cure for this condition. Those diagnosed are often treated with physical therapy. The doctors were also surprised that there was no reference to Albinism, in any of Nathans files. This is a congenital disorder characterized by the complete or partial absence of pigment in the skin, hair and eyes. This condition would explain his skin color or lack thereof. The only reference was to some documented incidents of name calling by the hospital staff. This would not however explain his pitch black eyes. The doctors could not find a medical reason for that. The other concern the doctors discussed was Nathans very small size. Test reveled that he had a severe case of Hyperthyroidism. They were amazed that he was doing as well as he was considering his files showed he had never received any type of medical treatment for this. Upon further investigation of his files, they realized he had never been tested or treated for anything. The doctors decided to start Nathan on a regiment of medication that would treat his thyroid problems along with steroids, collagen, a special high protein diet and physical therapy.

After all the results were in, Shaun called Jeff and asked if they could come in for a consultation. The doctors discussed the treatment schedule with Nathan's parents and requested there be no visitation whatsoever until they were convinced the treatments were working. The doctor said it may be a long time before we can let Nathan see anyone. We will let you know when it's time. We will send you progress reports on a quarterly basis. For the next two years, along with his regular treatment, Nathan was given steroids and taken to the weight room for several hours a day. Jeff continued to receive a quarterly report from the hospital informing them that Nathan was progressing very well with the treatment regimen and was finally gaining weight.

The family seemed to be on the right path for the first time in their life. Angel had made new friends, and so had her parents. The family had made new friends in the community and at work. They were being invited to cook outs. Angel had been invited to sleep over's. But, for some reason she declined. The parents had a meeting with Angel. They told her they thought it best not to mention Nathan. They thought it best, that if anyone asked if Angel had any brothers or sisters she would tell them no. They even told her since their families had disowned them if anyone asked about their relatives just to say that they were all dead. They even took all the pictures of Nathan and put them upstairs in the attic. They even considered burning just to make sure no one would know, but decided not to just in case one day Nathan might get to come home. This way if he saw the picture, at least he would know that they had not forgotten about him. As far as keeping Nathan a secret this was not a hard thing to do. They never talked about their past and the only people that knew them were the people in the community that they had moved to. Since they had new names no one could run a background check on them. Weeks turned into months. Finally things were looking like the family might actually have a chance at a normal life.

Jeff arrived home from work one afternoon after a very long day. He found the front door forced open. There Ruth lay on the bed beaten severely and raped, just like before in the exact same manner. Her driver's license and social security card had been stolen by the perpetrator again. The police were called to their house and conducted an extensive investigation but again to no avail. No clues, no suspects, nothing. This time this was enough. While Ruth lay in the hospital, Jeff called a company, and had high tech security cameras installed. These were not just regular cameras these had motion sensors, digital read out, infrared, night vision, and a playback that could be done from your cell phone.

Meaning, if you wanted to you could hit playback and see if anyone had come to the house or even walked in the yard. The playback was good for up to twenty four hours. After three days, Ruth was released from the hospital. Upon arriving at home she noticed a lot of strange new additions to the house and property. When she asked Jeff what was going on, he said, "We will not be run out of our house again. From now on, we can see if anyone tries to get in or has broken in while we were gone. Jeff called the police one more time to see if anything was new on the attack on his wife.

The detective in charge said to him, "We have no clues or evidence as of it, but rest easy as soon as we do and an arrest is made we will be glad to call you. Remember, your wife's drivers license and social security card will turn up again, it may be involving another case or crime but those items will turn up."

Three weeks later, Ruth had made a full recovery,

Jeff came in and said, "Honey, I have a surprise for you," He took her hand in his and walked outside. She began to cry when she saw what it was.

Chapter ten

WHEN SHE LOOKED DOWN the driveway there was the car packed and already for vacation. Jeff had gotten up early that morning and packed the bags for a two week vacation. They left and came back two weeks later. No one ever knew where they went. The family and Angel were getting ready to celebrate her birthday with her family and friends. They were getting ready for a wonderful weekend. The weekend was set. Just as soon as everyone came in that afternoon, they would go on a vacation.

The weekend was fantastic. They had plenty of food, fishing, and relaxation. When they returned home, they found a letter from the hospital where Nathan was. They put away all their weekend clothes, sat down, and opened the letter. The doctor requested they call him. They called and the doctor informed them that their son was well and ready to come home. All three felt their hearts stop beating.

They told the doctor they would be there in two days to get Nathan. There was very little talk on the drive. It had been a long time since they had last seen Nathan and they had no idea what to expect. They arrived at the hospital, taking their time walking in. The doctor met them at the door and said, "Welcome to our facility, are you ready to get your son?" They followed the doctor to the court yard. When they walked out into the yard they stopped suddenly. They couldn't see their son anywhere. The only thing they could see was the biggest, largest, man that they had ever seen in their life. His overall body mass was overwhelming, and he looked like he stood every bit of seven foot tall or better. His arms and hands were the size of nothing like they had ever seen before. He looked like someone had shaved a gorilla. With hair he could have been King Kong. He held out his arms and hands. When he did, they took three steps back.

The Doctor said, "This is your son." They could not believe that this mountain of a man was their son. Even if it had been awhile since they had last seen him, no one could change this much.

With a voice that had a sound as if someone was talking out of a thousand foot hole. He spoke, **"NO"**. They were shocked. The doctor said, "This is the only word he has spoken since his treatment began. A steady high protein diet along with exercise and weight lifting along and his medication has brought him to where he is now". As far as the prognosis for his future, only time will tell. The mere size of this mountain man was enough to intimidate anyone. I don't care who you are. After the initial shock of seeing his size was over, they did realize two things.

The two things that they did notice was that his skin color was still white as snow and his eyes were still pitch black with no emotion, just a solid black hole. They were very lucky they came in the van. He was so huge that he would not fit in the family car, even if they had taken the back seat out. They signed the release forms, and the Doctor escorted Nathan and his family to their van which was waiting outside.

The Doctor said, "Good luck". There was no way.

When he sat down in the van, you could hear the shocks buckle and cringed. During the entire trip back home, they were still in shock. They whispered very lightly to each other. What are we going to do? What will we do if he gets violent. There is no way we can stop him. They took their time so it would be late when they got home. They eased up in the drive way, so that they would not be seen. Luckily it was dark when they got home. I guess it was a good thing. The mere size would have freaked out the neighbors to no end. That night Nathan had to sleep in the floor. The bed was not big enough to hold this mountain.

Earlier in the week Ruth had ordered a brand new refrigerator. The call came in the next day that it had arrived at the store. The next morning, all four of them went in the van to pick up the refrigerator. The parents went inside the store and Angel and Nathan stayed in the van. They thought it best due to his size. Two delivery men were trying to pick up this large appliance, but were having a hard time. All of the sudden the van door opened. When Nathan got out of the van, you could hear the shocks sound with a sigh of relief. The two delivery men stopped and backed up. They didn't know whether to run, call for help or what to do. Nathan reached over with two hands and grabbed the appliance like me or you would grab a bag of groceries. And with ease, picked up the appliance and put it in the back of the delivery truck. No one said a word. I think they were just scared to say anything. The delivery truck followed the family home. All the way you could see the delivery men shaking their heads. You knew what the conservation was about. When arriving at home they rolled up the door to the truck and started to get the appliance. Again, Nathan reached over with both arms and picked up the appliance and walked in the house. The two men never said a word. They just got in their truck and left. Later that night it started raining. For the next three days it did nothing but rain. It looked like a monsoon. Streets were over flowing; septic tanks were flooded. It was the worst rain that this town had ever seen.

On the fourth day just about noon, the sounds of police cars and sirens, followed by an ambulance stopped in front of Jeff's house. Jeff and Ruth thought what now. Outside a lady was screaming. The police were over a steel grate with crow bars. Several other people were screaming. Jeff and Ruth slowly opened the door and walked outside to see what was going on. A little girl had walked out into the street and when she stepped off the curb, the water swept her under the side walk opening and down into the drain. Water was filling up, and the police could not get this large heavy steel grate removed from this death trap. Jeff ran back inside the house, grabbed his son Nathan, and through the door they ran. When Nathan ran out-side, people stopped screaming. They had never seen anything like this in their entire lives. Jeff took Nathan over to the steel grate and pointed to the little girl trapped in the hole. With one hand Nathan bent over and grabbed the steel grate and removed it from the hole. The little girl was saved. Maybe after all this time, he had changed. Now this gentle giant was a hero. By this time the news crew along with the entire street had filled the area. People were shouting and clapping and cheering. The story took first place, on the local news. Television and other reporters were having a field day. This gentle giant of whom no one knew was a hero. No one recognized Nathan, but, when pictures of the rest of the family were shown on TV, someone did recognize them. Phone calls started coming in from some of the places they had lived.

All of a sudden this hero was not a hero anymore. Now with his size it looked like bad luck would have its way again. Word had gotten out about who this gentle giant really was and about all the awful things that he had done. The neighborhood was on alert. Two days later the sound of silence was broken when a scream came from the house next door where the gentle giant lived. The police were called. In the back yard there stood Angel. Twenty feet in front of Angel was Nathan and stretched over a clothes line were two cats with their tails tied together. The blood and guts were gory. When the police converged to the back yard they ordered Nathan to drop the rope. The only word he could speak was **"NO"**. At that point he started walking towards the officers. This time they told him to stop and drop the rope. Nathan replied **"NO"** again. This time one officer drew his tactical taser. For those of you that are not familiar with a tactical taser it shoots two fish hook barbs attached by a wire connected to a gun which will administer fifty thousand volts for several seconds. Nathan kept walking towards the officers. Once again the officers shouted stop. Nathan replied, "**NO.**" This time the first officer shot Nathan with the taser, nothing happened. The fifty thousand volts had no effect on him what so ever. The second officer drew his taser and shot for another fifty thousand volts, nothing. He kept walking towards the officers. By this time four other officers had arrived at the scene. It took six officers and two neighbors to tackle him and get him on the ground. But there was still another problem. The hand cuffs would not come close to fitting. One officer noticed a large chain in the car port. They took the chain and tied his hands and arms. They took the cuffs and ran them through the links on the chain to lock them in place. Now there was another problem. He would not fit in the patrol car. They had to borrow a truck to take him to jail. He was charged with cruelty to animals and resisting arrest. This time the family hired a well known lawyer to make sure what happened last time would not happen again. Nathan was placed in a cell by himself. The other prisoners were very scared of this gentle giant. The day of the trial the courtroom was filled with standing room only. If nothing else, everyone including the news and reporters were wanting to catch a glimpse of the man, who tortured cats but saved a little girl.

The trial started again, the DA was hot and ready. He told of a child who was destined to kill. He brought up all the past events, and history from day one. Again, Nathan's lawyer just sat there. Nathan's family looked at him asked him to do something. He did not. When the judge called for recess, Nathan's family was in an uproar. They confronted the lawyer. He simply looked at them and said, "Trust me," and walked off. After the DA had completed his summation the lawyer called for six witnesses. One by one he called each of the officers in and asked each Officer to give a detailed report on what happened. One by one they did. Nathan's lawyer had their entire report in front of him as they gave a play by play description of the event. After all six officers had given their testimony Nathan's lawyer turned to the judge and asked for a mistrial. The courtroom exploded. Extra officers were called in to handle the unruly crowd. Why on God's green earth would you call for a mistrial.

The lawyer simply said, "Throughout all the commotion, at no time did any of the officers while at the scene or in the jail give my client the "**Miranda act.**" They never read him his rights".

The judge looked at the DA and looked at the Lawyer and Nathan and simply said. **"You're free to go"**. The judge ordered the court room cleared except for the six officers who arrested Nathan. Let's just say the officers and chief got a major butt chewing for their screw up.

The judge told the Officers. "If you **ever** bring that freak in here again. You had better have your T's crossed and your I's dotted. Or, I will have your badges. And, I will dot your eyes with time in jail.

Once back at the Police department. The chief took up where the judge left off. The chief said, "The next time you plan to bring Nathan in **don't!"**

Around the house there's no way to describe the scene but chaotic. Neighbors filled the street; phone calls flooded the house. Again, it was time to move.

But where could they go. After all the reporters, news and publicity it would be nearly impossible to find a place with a future.

Chapter eleven

THE FAMILY WAS LOOKING for a new place to
move when a knock was heard at the door. Jeff went
to the door with a hammer in his hand. It was Ray
C, the dad of the little girl that Nathan had saved.
He heard what was going on and offered the family
a place to stay in an extra house on his property.
This was the least he could do for Nathan saving his
daughters life. They accepted his offer. Three weeks
went by. The owner of the house offered Nathan a
job working on his farm feeding cows, and mowing
the grass. It seemed if the media would let things die
down, they might have a chance at life again. Things
were good again. Three months had gone by. The
media was fading and so were the on lookers. Another
two weeks went by the media was gone. On lookers
had all but disappeared. There were a few minor
problems with the neighbors complaining about their
houses being broken into. But nothing was taken.

Again, the family had a possible shot at life. "Calm before the storm"

Early one morning a call to 911 was received. The police were sent to the address of 666 Cannibal Lane. This was the address of Ray C, the father of the little girl that Nathan had saved. The police went to the corner of the house. There stood Nathan with a push mower. In front of the push mower was the owner of the house, Ray C, lying on the ground in a pool of blood. It appeared that Nathan had gone on a wild rampage, Ray's right hand and right foot and leg were cut to ribbons. There Nathan stood still holding on to the mower. The man or what was left of him, was lying on the ground. Ray C was the man who had given Nathan and his family a place to stay. The officers had already called for backup knowing what had happened last time Nathan was involved with officers. The officers told Nathan to drop the lawnmower. Nathan turned towards the officers with the mower still in his hands. Nathan took two steps in the officer's direction. The two officers drew their weapons. Again, one officer shouted, "Nathan, drop the mower and lay down!" Nathan dropped the mower and turned with his bloody hands facing forward and his arms out stretched. He looked at the officers and took one more step toward them. One of the officers there had already seen the strength that Nathan possessed. He was one of the officers at the scene where the little girl was trapped in the drain. When Nathan took another step, six shots rang out. All six shots by the officer found their mark, right in the center of Nathan's chest. Nathan fell to his knees and looked down at his bullet ridden shirt. Nathan got up and took two more steps towards the officers. Four more shots rang out. The chief had hit his mark. All four shots had hit Nathan, two shots in each of Nathan's upper legs. One more time Nathan fell to his knees, blood pouring from his shirt and pants. Nathan never made a sound. He looked at the officers and started to get up. At that moment, other officers who had arrived at the scene ran and tackled him from behind. In all, six officers were on top of Nathan kicking and beating him. After a few moments they were able to subdue him. Nathan was so huge that when the medics arrived, they requested the police bring a truck to take Nathan to the hospital. He would not fit on the stretcher. The medics stopped the bleeding of Nathan's bullet ridden body. As far as Ray C, he was dead. With a police escort leading the truck and two police cars following, Nathan was taken to the nearest trauma center. It took some doing, but Nathan was removed from the truck. With the help of several people, Nathan was taken into the ER. The doctor on call was astonished that Nathan had ten bullet wounds. Yet, Nathan showed no sign of pain. After xrays, it was determined not to remove any of the bullets due to Nathan's massive size. Four officers were assigned to guard Nathan 24/7 in the hospital.

Three days later, the doctor said, "It's a miracle, but Nathan is ready to be released into police custody." Outside the hospital there had to have been 300 people wanting to catch a glimpse of Nathan. An armored car was used to transport Nathan to the jail. Behind the police escort, there was a stretch of cars with people wanting to see Nathan that looked to be a mile long. When the armored car arrived at the jail, it was met with two dozen officers, all fully armed in riot gear, with shot guns. This time they were not taking any chances. Inside the jail, special preparations were made just to house Nathan. He was being assigned to a jail cell by himself that had been equipped with three very large log chains. Two chains for his ankles and one that would be placed around his neck.

Nathan's parents contacted the same lawyer for Nathan. After meeting with Jeff and Ruth on two separate occasions, the lawyer told them not to worry. The day of the trial finally arrived. Nathan would be tried as an adult. When Nathan was brought into the courtroom, a silence fell over the entire place. His mammoth size was unbelievable, and he was still being restrained with the log chains from head to toe. The DA told the judge that if Nathan got loose in the court room, it would be chaos for all. This time the DA was ready. He was seeking the death penalty. He brought up everything he could find on Nathan. The icing on the cake was the photographs taken at the crime scene. No doubt about it, Nathan was done for. The entire time during the trial Nathan's lawyer would say "no questions at this time". Finally the DA was done. This was an air tight case. Nathan's lawyer approached the jury. The lawyer presented a cigar box that was found in Ray C's bedroom. He asked the Judge to admit the cigar box and the contents there in into evidence. The DA had no objections. And so it was. He opened the cigar box and showed the contents to the jury and court room along with numerous police reports from other areas. The DA shouted, "That does not give him the right to commit murder." The last four pieces of paper the lawyer presented were two sets of Drivers license and two social security cards, both having the same name. Ruth . . . . the police report was where Ray C had been charged at least a half dozen times with rape and assault on women, but had never been convicted. The cigar box also contained a dozen or more ID cards of other women who had been raped and beaten. The assailant was never found in those cases. The lawyer also brought to the jury's attention, that in a lot of cases the perpetrator will keep the Drivers license and other personal effects of his victims as a trophy so he can reflect back on his crimes and misadventures. One by one, the lawyer called medics and officers to the stand to testify. It was obvious that Ray C was the man who had raped and beaten Ruth, on two different occasions many years ago. So I guess Ray C didn't forget after all about being made fun of when he worked for Jeff a long time ago.

After Nathan's lawyer finished his questions, he stood up and asked the judge for a mistrial. The courtroom exploded. Word of the requested mistrial hit outside the court house. In the street it was a riot. Except for about 40 to 50 people who were dressed in black holding up lighters shouting "**Nathan**", "**Nathan**", "**Nathan**".

Back inside the courtroom the judge finally restored order, then asked why a mistrial. Nathan's lawyer said, "Your honor, through all the commotion, sirens, police, gunshots, media and everything else aforementioned, at no time was Nathan ever read the **Miranda act**". There is no record from any officer saying one word to that fact; therefore, in the realm of justice, a mistrial is the only course of action." The judge called for a break and ordered the DA and Nathan's lawyer to his chambers. Fifteen minutes later court resumed and the judge declared a mistrial due to the fact that no Miranda was ever given. Nathan would be required to wear an ankle bracelet and not be allowed to leave his house.

The judge said, "Ray C said, "I won't forget".

The judge looked at the police chief and his officers and said, "I won't forget either. Ray C said he had been made fun of, well you've made a mockery of my court". The judge was not a happy camper. He called the police chief back to his chambers and dismissed the court room. Two hours later, the police chief exited the judge's chambers. He had to tighten his belt four notches due to the fact that he had received a good butt chewing. The chief called his officers in for a meeting. We can't use the words that echoed from the walls. But, the bottom line was don't ever bring Nathan back here again. The next time you get a call to 666 Cannibal Lane. Make it your last, or it will be your last day you will ever wear that uniform again. Don't go by yourself. We will all go.

Nathan was returned to his home by a police escort. Nathan arrived home wearing his ankle bracelet and was confined to the house until the court could figure out what to do. The neighbors, furious with the judge's decision, stormed out of the court room and followed the police escort and Nathan home along with other on lookers. One neighbor decided to take a trip for the weekend. They thought it would be a good time to get away from all the madness and chaos. Maybe things would settle down. The thing was Nathan was free. The judge had the ankle bracelet put on Nathan just to keep tabs on his location for the time being and maybe to ease the minds of the public.

Three days later. The police were called to the house were Nathan lived. When the same six officers and the chief went in the house, they just looked at Nathan. All six officers were horrified at what they saw. They looked at each other, drew their weapons, and emptied their weapons into Nathan. The chief was not about to take a chance on another behind the door session with the judge. This time Nathan was dead. His body was riddled with dozens of rounds. What the officers saw was Nathan standing over his parents with an axe. When Nathan turned around and took one step towards them with his arms stretched out palms forward and blood dripping from his hands they had all made the decision to fire, unloading their weapons. This was the final straw. Jeff and Ruth lay dead on the floor. Above the parents hung over the ceiling fan, again, were two cats with their tails tied together. The scene inside the house was horrific with blood and other carnage. We wanted to print a copy of the pictures in this book. But, the scene was way too graphic.

Now was another question to be answered. Where was Angel? Once again here came the reporters, on-lookers, and fans of Nathan. They swarmed the house like bees after honey. Dozens of on lookers stood outside the house where Nathan was thought to be dead. One group of 30-40 people all wearing black with hoods covering their faces were gathered together holding lighters high in the air chanting **Nathan, Nathan, Nathan**. At the moment when the coroner and officers removed Nathan from the house, they all raised their hands and began to sing, "na na na na, na na na Na, hey, hey, good bye". Extra officers were called in to control the crowd because of the singing. The neighbors in the surrounding areas were outside the property. This time they wanted to see the so called gentle giant. They demanded to see the body. They wanted positive proof that this killer, this monster, was, in fact, dead. The neighbors didn't just want a burial. They wanted to see Nathan burned in an open field, and sent back to **hell** from which he came. It took several hours to secure the scene. After all the evidence was collected and the corner pronounced Nathan and his parents dead they were transferred to the morgue. Finally there would be no more. No more tortured animals, no more dead people. No more Nathan. Finally there would be peace on earth.

Angel as a teenager.

Angel as a 2 year old

Chapter twelve

THE NEXT MORNING THE police were called to the morgue. How could it be possible? Nathan was gone. Officers from across the county converged on the morgue. The corner swore up and down Nathan was dead. A search began county wide. A call came in from one officer. Nathan had been spotted. Law enforcement county wide converged on Nathan's location. Upon arrival they got out of their vehicles loaded for bear or in this case, Nathan. When they saw Nathan, it was obviousthat he was dead. Either someone or numerous people had broken into the morgue. They had taken Nathan to the edge of an abandoned cemetery. It was carnage. Someone had dismembered his body in four separate spots, poured gasoline and yellow paint over his body. Took a match and burned his remains. A note was placed at the edge of the flames. The note simply stated. **Lucifer he's yours! Burn in hell**. Once again, Nathan's follower's stood at the road side singing. "sha na Na na na na na na hey hey good by. This went on for hours.

With all the carnage and happenings everyone had forgotten about Angel. A search of the house and grounds revealed Angel was nowhere to be found. An officer called from Angel's bedroom. Angel had left a note on her bathroom mirror. Angel, by the grace of God, had gone to check out one of the local colleges. She had escaped the wrath of Nathan. The reporters swarmed the house and farm. People once again, stood outside the house cheering the beast was dead. Finally **Satan** was dead. By the time the neighbors returned home from vacation, all was cleared except for the yellow tape left by the police. Angel had already moved into the dorm at college. Finally all was well.

PEACE ON EARTH

Once the police officers secured the scene, they took pictures and waited on the coroner to arrive. When the coroner arrived, he started collecting Nathan's body parts to be returned to the morgue again.

The chief spoke up and asked the coroner. "Are you sure he is dead this time?"

The corner turned and with a sarcastic grin on his face and said, "**Hell,** with Nathan you can never be sure". Your officers shot him with fifty rounds. Someonetook his body was dismembered in four sections, saturated with yellow paint and gasoline. He was set on fire".

The chief spoke up and said. "Yes sir, under normal conditions that would be enough for anybody. But, then who ever said Nathan was normal". They had not even had time to clear the scene. The word was out. It did not take long. The area was covered with gothic on lookers and dozens of Nathan's fans. It was not hard to distinguish one from the other. All of Nathan's fans were dressed in black with black hoods. The majority of them were carrying lighted candles. All of them were singing. "sha na, na, na, na, na, na, na, hey, hey, good bye". The chief sent one officer to stand between the two crowds to help keep peace. As the coroner was trying to put Nathan's body back in the hearse one more time numerous fans were actually trying to touch Nathan's body. Some were even trying to grab a piece of his clothing and even a body part for a souvenir. When the hearse left the scene, some of Nathan's fans stayed at the scene. Others followed the hearse.

All who followed, were shouting, **"Nathan, Nathan, Nathan"**. As if they were expecting him to get up and jump out of the back of the hearse. The coroner wasn't too sure himself. Just as a precaution, he kept his hand on the hearse door. If Nathan did get back up, as far as the coroner was concerned, Nathan could have the hearse, because he would be gone. The way the coroner looked at it with Nathan you just could not be sure one way or the other.

They finally arrived back at the morgue. Nothing happened. Nathan's fans waited all night just in case he did come back to life. You would think with the death of Nathan's parent's and Nathan locked up in the morgue with armed officers, and Angel nowhere to be found, peace would be a sure thing.

The next morning, the sounds of sirens echoed down the street. This little sleepy town had not seen this much excitement since the police chief's dog was beaten up by the neighbor's cat, five years ago. With a convoy of vehicles following the sirens, the destination was obvious. They were going back to Nathan's house one more time. As the fire department, police officers, medics and a variety of fans and gothic on-lookers emerged from their cars, they saw Nathan's house fully engulfed with flames bursting through the roof. No one was making an effort to put out the fire. The police chief just stood there at the front gate. All he had to say was. "Enough is enough, "**Burn baby burn!**".. They watched the house burn to the ground and no one lifted a finger. After a while the fire department and police officers left. By the end of the day there was only a hand full of people waiting for something else unexpected to happen. It never did. By the next morning everyone was gone. There were rumors the fire was arson. But, no investigation was ever done. There were also rumors that before the house went up in flames, that maybe some reporters snuck in the house to acquire some souvenirs. The big item was photos of Angel and Nathan. Since Ruth had a photo shop, they were sure to find hundreds of photos of Angel and Nathan. The investigators were disappointed to find only four pictures of the children, two of Angel and two of Nathan. Those four photos are shown in this book. Someone asked about school pictures. For whatever reason, every time school photos were taken Angel and Nathan always managed to be out. Therefore, there were no school photos ever taken. No photos were ever found of Jeff or Ruth. As far as the fire was concerned, everything inside the house was completely destroyed with the exception of two items, a picture frame, with a log cabin inside of it and a wooden plaque under it that read "REMEMBER". The wooden plaque and the picture did not have any fire damage to them at all. Everything else was completely destroyed. In fact neither of these two items had any damage to them at all.

The next morning, the police were called to Cannibal Lane. This time they were told to report to neighbor's house across the road. They told the police that they had something they needed to see. Before the neighbors went out of town, they installed an audio and video surveillance system in their house. They plugged the tape in and you could hear two cats screeching as if they were watching their nine lives slip away. There was a silhouette of a person carrying the two cats. Finally on tape was the proof that everyone was waiting on. Caught in the act, there was Angel, Nathan's sister, carrying the two cats. As soon as the officers saw the video, they called their chief. The chief and four officers converged on Angel's dorm room. They entered the room with their weapons drawn not knowing what they would encounter or find. Upon entering the room, the odor of blood and decay seemed to flood their noses and mouths. One by one they cleared the room looking for Angel. The closer they got to the back room the stronger the odor and taste were. The only room left was Angel's bathroom. When they reached her door, it was obvious that something was not right. Something bad had happened here. With their guns still drawn they shouted, "Angel, come out with your hands up". There was no response. Two more times they shouted for Angel to come out. Again, there was no response. The chief gave the order to open the bathroom door. When the officers opened the door a swarm of green blow flies covered them as if they were looking for relief to get out of the room. Just as soon as the officers removed the flies from their faces and bodies, they could see why. "Oh my God", the chief screamed. There stretched across the curtain, was what appeared to be six cats or what was left of them. Blood and other animal parts were dripping on the floor from the saturated linen. On each corner of the shower rod was the head of a cat. Each cat has its tongue stretched completely out as far as possible from their mouths. Due to the carnage and the odor, one of the officers became sick, threw up, and fainted. The other officers picked up their friend and ran towards the front door. They were also feeling weak and sick. The chief still with his gun drawn entered Angel's bathroom. When he looked at the mirror, he was totally horrified at what he saw. A note had been left on the mirror. It appeared to be written in cat's blood. He took pictures of the note. This is what was written.

Behold these eyes
How lifeless how still
Destined for immortality
Destined to kill
Where blood did run
Through his body and veins
He's returned to **hell**
In which he will reign,

You burned my brother's body
Showing hatred and sin
You forgot one thing
You forgot his twin,
Enjoy your revenge
Enjoy your misgivings
Not all what you see
Are things of believing?
Remember those people and cats
From whom saw slaughter
The jokes on you
I'm Satans Daughter.

The word came across the radio, and numerous police, fire, medics and responders came running, along with dozens of reporters and citizens throughout the area. The first three responders that arrived at the dorm did not see the other officer standing at the corner, so they went in the building. As they were entering the dorm, other units and people arrived. As they were getting out of their vehicles and approaching the scene the first three responders came running back out. They were gagging and severely throwing up. Two of those responders, named Adam and Brad, were used to taking the gory and bloody scenes that no one else wanted. When they saw their reactions and the effect it had on them they knew right then they did not need to go inside. By this time the odor and smell of blood had reached the front door.

People who were walking on the porch decided they did not need to go in the dorm. Word hit the community and the next thing you know, it was a circus. Everyone from miles around wanted to see. Reporters flooded the area telling of what carnage had been done. Pictures of the scene were shown. Within a few minutes the story was all over the county. Some of the reporters figured the police and responders that had entered the dorm were trying to hide something. They did not think the scene could be as bad as everyone was saying.

Some reporters tried keeping the police busy while their friends snuck in. Within a few seconds they were also running from the house throwing up. The tales of the gruesome slaughter of cats and the horrific murder that Angel had committed spread like wildfire. A state wide search was issued for Angel. Photos of her were plastered everywhere. The scene inside the dorm was nowhere near what the reports described. They could not even come close. A reward was issued, not just by the police, but by the animal rights group that had arrived. They all wanted a part of this so called Angel. Not only were the gothic seekers and satanic people there, it was believed that they were there to help Angel try to escape. When the broadcast hit the police band, no one recognized the names of the family, but just as soon as the pictures hit the fax, phone calls started coming in from different police stations in the areas in which the family had previously lived. Their real names were now known. Other police departments started calling giving their updates and status of what went on in their communities along with the names of the family. The doctors were soon flooded with reports asking about the family and Nathan.

One doctor answered his call for an interview. When asked about Nathan and his family, the doctor showed one picture. It was Nathan holding his hands out palms up. The doctor told them Nathan's only spoken word was **"no"**. To cover his own ass, the doctor told the reporters he told the parents and police that he thought Nathan was innocent all along. I had doubts of Nathan being guilty from the start but no one would hear of it. With that being said, the only other thing I can say is "no comment". To this day, twice a year six black roses are left on Nathan's grave site, one time in the morning at 5 am, and the again in the evening at 5 pm, on his birthday Friday the 13th. Another strange fact just in case you missed it. Nathan died on the same day he was born, Friday the13th. Numerous people and law enforcement have tried catching the person or persons involved, but to no avail. Some say it's Angel. Some say its fans of Nathan and Angel. Some even say it's **Satan** himself.

I would give you the name of the town and cemetery where all this took place. But I was strongly advised not to. They say that good cannot exist without evil. For this community evil will exist forever. They fear the day Angel will return. They keep their animals locked up at night. No one knows why Angel singled out cats for most of her destruction. Some of the rumors are that it might be hereditary or a premonition from past events from long ago, but that has never been proven to be an actual fact, **(or has it)**. Remember Jeff's brother, Dave, the one that overdosed on drugs and thought he was a cat. No one knows why Angel let Nathan take the fall for all of her actions. The reporters say it was just **the devil in her**.

Remember at the first of the book. We said it was a small world and how some events or people would encounter each other throughout history. This book has given you several points of how life changing events cross the paths of others again and again, so if your animals are acting stranger than usual or your cats have come up missing, don't worry Angel just might be in your neighborhood.

The one thing that we may never know is, did Nathan really have a nerve disease and medical Problems, or was he in fact, the devils son.

To this day Nathan's sister Angel has never been found. Just curious, any new neighbors lately. Don't let your cats walk loose on the street and remember to check your clothes lines.

The end.

Chapter thirteen

O R MAYBE NOT.